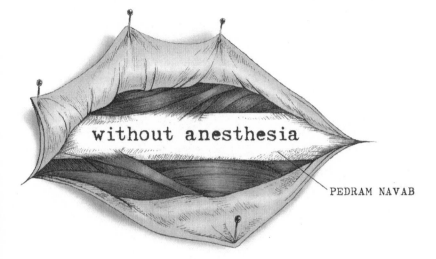

without anesthesia

PEDRAM NAVAB

© 2015 copyright by Pedram Navab

First black and white print edition. All rights reserved.

ISBN: 978-1-937543-70-9

Printed in the United States of America. No part of this book may be used or reproduced in any manner whatsoever without written permission from the publisher, except in the case of brief quotations embodied in critical articles and reviews. For information please email: questions@jadedibisproductions.com

Published by Jaded Ibis Press, sustainable literature by digital means™, an imprint of Jaded Ibis Productions, LLC, Seattle, Washington USA.

Cover and interior art by Yalda Zakeri. Author photo by Filip Milenkovic. Book design by Debra Di Blasi.

This book is available in multiple formats. Visit our website for more information: jadedibisproductions.com

Without Anesthesia

a novel

Pedram Navab

art by Yalda Zakeri

Jaded Ibis Press
sustainable literature by digital means™
an imprint of Jaded Ibis Productions
Seattle • Hong Kong • Boston

"...A letter can always not arrive at its destination."

—Jacques Derrida
Le Facteur de la Verite

"She is selected, she will be overtaken."

—Søren Kierkegaard
The Seducer's Diary

The First Cut

Dear Tess,

We cut you up today. I was the first to go. We played that old childhood game of rock-paper-scissors and although my intention was to lose, the scissors made me winner (does no one choose rock anymore, that stalwart Sisyphean element?). How ironic this all was. I won with dull scissors and they made me cut you first with a sharp razor. Scalpel Blade No. 11, to be exact. I couldn't bear the thought that you were looking at me, slice you, mince you like meat. So I draped those hazy eyes with heavy, white, formaldehyde-drenched sheets and began cutting. Please forgive me. Again and again, I'll ask for your forgiveness. The skin was so tight at first. I couldn't cut. But they taunted me, put more pressure on her, dig deeper, they shouted, be a real fucking man, until the skin finally gave in. A sharp gash in the abdomen. It felt that your skin was glued to you as I tried to then pry it with those sweaty hands, swimming in latex gloves. So sticky, your skin. Like chicken. And, then, more chunks of yellow fat and connective tissue underneath. It reminded me of mother's custard pie. Hardened crust, but so soft inside. At last, the rectus abdominis muscle was visible, angled perfectly. Those killers cheered me on. Oh, fuck yeah. Fuck yeah! Cut, brave soldier, cut. The first cut was successful. And then they started to clear away the fat even more and extricate that muscle until it was isolated. I had cut you first and, for that, there is no excuse. This was my first cut of you, my first glance into your inside.

Your friend,
Adrien

Dear Tess,

We cut you up some more today. Maybe you liked it, I can't tell for sure. You are now so open to me, to us. So open, but so concealed. You couldn't be further away. I can tell. Your glassy eyes roll themselves away as if your thoughts are elsewhere. As if you were bored with us and all that we had planned for you. No. You should listen. There are things in store for you. Yes, as you may have guessed, horrible things. I am so sorry, Tess. The others are working on you day and night, exposing more muscles and nerves. Your yellow fat surrounds us but, now and again, they manage to toss it into that filthy bucket. That bucket now holds so much of you, pieces of you, skin that is now so sallow and wilted and nerves and veins, which were accidentally cut. You know, they even cursed at you. For having such a complicated body, and muscles and nerves that are so tenuous and difficult to locate. Fuck her, they said. Fuck her. But she has a name, I said. Tess. Fuck Tess, then.

Forever your friend,
Adrien

Their two bodies lay side by side, unperfected. Naked, they were the mismatched pieces of a jigsaw puzzle. Their torsos touched, but the angle was not quite right for a symmetrical union. The connection was botched. The alliance of the parts looked grotesque. There it was. The striated belly of the older body was annexed to a pouch, a colostomy bag, saturated with bilious fluid. If one looked closer, microscopically, he could almost see the density of the microbes that populated and germinated in this vast sewer of a fluid. The overwhelming nausea that this scene depicted was too much. But the younger body, pale, lean, muscular, with hints of breasts, also looked distorted somehow, as if it had become part of the other and required it for sustenance. There was nothing mathematical or clean about this juxtaposition but, yet, it intuitively made sense. That these oddities should coexist, that this was now the natural order of the universe.

The tepid smell of decay had begun to embrace them. There were three now, Death the unexpected guest. Death glanced around the room, taking in the scene in which she was now placed. It was the final act, just as she liked it. She smoked her cigarette, puffing slowly, taking this all in. Her fedora hat was slanted, partially concealing her eyes. She laughed. Her misshapen and chipped teeth gleamed white against the black hat. A hint of sadness, however, shone in her white pupils, which never reflected anything or anyone. Death had expected this, but not so soon. She had planned to spend the day by the ocean, eyeing the victim she was prepared to see drown. She had no control over these deaths that now lay at her black corseted shoes. It must have some significance she thought, and let the ash fall on the older body. She always let the ash fall.

The ceiling light flickered. It cast its sallow hue on the white faces, which would soon take on their own shades of yellows and blues. The blinds, closed, would conceal for at least a few hours this macabre union. The silence was intermittently being interrupted by the flickering, neon lights. The bag, hung overhead, once having contained intravenous fluids, was now shriveled, no longer purposeful. It had given all it could. It could give no more.

Death made her exit, briefly stopping to crush the cigarette with her high-

heeled pumps. Her left eyebrow peaked. Her lips puckered. She applied classic red lipstick. Recently, she had tried to look the part of a femme fatale when she crushed her dead victims. Death always looked good, even when she was cast as an extra.

KNOW THAT YOU'LL EVENTUALLY DO IT. UNDERSTAND THAT THEY WON'T LET YOU LEAVE UNTIL YOU MAKE THE FIRST CUT. GRAB THAT RAZOR. CUT HER. IMAGINE THAT YOU'RE CUTTING YOUR FATHER WHOM YOU FUCKING HATE. THINK BACK TO THAT TIME WHEN YOUR FATHER SLAPPED YOU AND KILLED THE WOLF THAT YOU FELT SORRY FOR RIGHT IN FRONT OF YOU WITH THE HOT RED BLOOD FLOWING FROM ITS BODY AND INTO YOUR HANDS. CUT THIS CADAVER AS IF SHE WERE YOUR FATHER. DON'T LET THEM SEE YOU SWEAT BECAUSE YOUR LATEX GLOVES ARE ALREADY DRENCHED WITH SWEAT. BUT REALIZE THAT THEY HAVE ALREADY SEEN THIS. KNOW THAT THEY KNOW THAT YOU'RE SO NERVOUS ABOUT CUTTING HER. CONCENTRATE ON HER BODY. MAKE SURE THAT YOU'RE AT LEAST CUTTING THE RIGHT MUSCLE, THE RECTUS ABDOMINIS, BECAUSE THERE'S NOTHING WORSE THAN HAVING TO MAKE THE FIRST CUT AND CUTTING THE WRONG MUSCLE. PRETEND THAT YOU'RE FUCKING STRONG WHEN ALL THAT YOU WANT TO DO NOW IS GO HOME AND EAT ONE OF MOTHER'S CUSTARD PIES AND LIE ON THE COUCH AND FORGET THAT YOU'RE LOOKING AT A CORPSE THAT ONCE RESEMBLED YOU, THAT ONCE LOOKED, BREATHED, AND TALKED AS YOU ARE DOING NOW. TRY NOT TO CUT YOUR FINGER WITH SCALPEL BLADE NO. 11 BECAUSE THE BLOOD WILL JUST REMIND YOU THAT YOU'RE LIVING AND THAT, AT SOME POINT, WILL DIE JUST LIKE THIS CADAVER DID. TELL THE OTHERS THAT THIS CADAVER WHOM THEY'RE CURSING HAS A NAME, AND THAT HER NAME IS TESS, BECAUSE YOU SAW A TATTOO WITH THAT NAME ON THE BACK OF HER NECK. PRETEND THAT YOU DON'T CARE ABOUT HER, THIS CADAVER NAMED TESS, ALTHOUGH YOU FEEL THAT YOU'RE ALREADY IN LOVE WITH HER IN SOME WAY, BECAUSE IT ALL STARTS LIKE THAT, AND WILL EVENTUALLY UNRAVEL WHEN THE KILLERS KNOW WHERE YOUR WEAKNESS LIES AND THOSE FUCKERS CAN USE THAT WEAKNESS AGAINST YOU AT ANY TIME.

TESS GAZED INTENTLY at the woman who had just been diagnosed with a panic disorder. The woman had streaks of grey in her disheveled hair and creased lines on her forehead. Despite these imperfections, she resembled a mannequin, but one that had been resold, repackaged, and recycled, and made to conform to today's fashions despite the short shelf life. She was probably in her late-forties, although she looked at least ten years older. Discrete shades of blotched purple and blue were present on her cheeks, more prominent on the left. Tess couldn't see the woman's torso, but imagined bruise after blotched bruise, like on her cheeks. The left side of her head revealed a superficial contusion. There was no doubt about it. This patient had been battered. She had been repeatedly battered.

The woman was sitting in one of the old vanilla-colored, plastic Hasbro-looking chairs lining the corridor and staring intently at the wall. She had a waxy immobility about her, as if she could be molded into whatever shape Tess desired. The immobility was striking. The patient had been recently administered 2 mg of Ativan and her behavior had completely changed within half an hour. She had come into the ER as such a wreck, hyperventilating and tachycardic, and Tess had internalized these symptoms as her own. Tess imagined herself battered and whipped, like the woman had been, just as hard, even harder, her face and body against the cane, rope, or knuckles of that man, and she hungrily savored the coldness, cruelty, and intensity of that pain. She envisioned the patient's other body parts and crevices with similar marks of a beating and wanted to deeply palpate these as if they had been transferred onto her own body. Through the patient's demeanor, Tess had partially internalized the patient's sweating, her palpable heart rate, and her hyperventilation as if she herself were undergoing a panic attack. Tess was keenly aware and well-versed in the power of biofeedback, but rather than using it for her own good, she was using it now to punish herself and empathize with this patient. But the calmness was so different. Tess couldn't feel this yet.

It was her first rotation in medical school and her first few days in the ER. Tess wanted to wrap herself around the patient's symptoms as if she were tightly wrapped cellophane. She knew that there was always a possibility of being stretched so far that she would tear, of having her feelings stripped from her so that she no longer felt anything, but, now, she needed to feel this. Tess needed to mirror the patient's own symptoms back to her, and let her know that a bond existed between them, that Tess was feeling what the woman was feeling at that moment.

The senior resident, Abigail, had asked Tess to assist with the discharge of this patient. Tess saw this as a perfect opportunity to feel the effects of the Ativan, and, by extension, the patient's own calmness, and strike a conversation with the woman. In this way, she justified her actions of taking a few of these tablets from the patient's plastic orange bottle when discharging her.

The small, white tablet had almost melted in Tess's sweaty palms. She had stared at it for a while and placed it in her mouth before it disintegrated. She had not swallowed the tablet, but rather chewed it whole to feel the bitterness, every last molecule that comprised it. The Ativan tablet worked within her almost instantly. Her breathing slowed, and her heart was beating a little slower. She felt the onslaught of a gentle tidal wave that was carrying her away into a cold, deep, white ocean where she could no longer feel anything.

During the calmness that invaded her body, Tess realized that she was so different from the other medical students who wanted to get the job done and go about their business as efficiently as possible. She only ever wanted, this. This thing that had no name and nothing to articulate. Like a tattered old sweater with torn seams, it clung to her. She couldn't let go of it. She needed it as much as it needed her. If it could only speak to her and communicate what it needed. But it didn't speak, and wouldn't speak for a while. This thing for which she had no name.

Without Anesthesia

Dear Tess,

We tugged on your heartstrings today. Those chordae tendinae, tendons that connect muscles to heart valves. These string-like, orchestral things were solemnly playing their own tune for you, funereal to be sure, but also majestically extraterrestrial. And you were singing your own elegy from above. I listened very closely. It was so beautifully tragic. I cried. Wept again and again, but I didn't let them see my tears. We explored those fleshy beams of yours, the trabeculae carneae, irregular muscular columns that give the heart its character. In following these caverns, I envisioned a shrunken eye formed by these numerous fleshy bands. It was really there, looking at me, look at your heart. I felt like a voyeur. Not until then did I realize the undertaking we had commenced. We were not only looking at you. We were looking at your innards, your most private possessions to which you yourself were not even privy. God, what had we done to you, you poor rag doll! Underneath the eye, I saw that numerous chordae tendinae had attempted to come together to create lips for you. They were unsuccessful. The whole thing looked lousy. There they were, ruptured and whip-lashed, looking like a pair of sardonic lips, mocking you for what you had become. Was I hallucinating a story within your heart, reading what was not there? The nuns dissected Sister Clara de Montefalco's body in the year of the Lord 1308. They read in her heart the story of the flagellated Christ. I read in your heart a story that was over before it had started.

Yours truly,
Adrien

Without Anesthesia

Dear Tess,

We crushed your heart today. Mitral and tricuspid valves, atria
and ventricles, all asundered with our sharp scalpels. It was so
small, smaller than I had imagined, this heart of yours. It seemed
that it had shrunk from all the pain you may have endured. The
blood had been drained from it. It was so white, like an apparition.
All sorts of arteries and veins were jutting out of it, looking like
pipes and sewers in a house. We followed the paths laid out by your
heart, but it was so complicated. I couldn't get it right. Where did it
lead? Was there an attic or basement in this house of yours? Any
terrible secrets to be kept there? I was looking for a sign to figure
out this heart of yours. Whom did you love? Was it broken before,
before we had tapped it? Did it skip a beat now and then? I couldn't
find a thing and the others kept dissecting, cutting more. Her
heart's even fucked-up, they said. Like the rest of her. So cruel to
you. But now at least you don't have a heart with which to feel this
cruelty. We had broken your heart today and there was no way to
mend it. It was all fucked.

Sorry,
Adrien

My Dear Tess,

It breaks my heart to see your heart crushed like this. They have
somehow managed to sever the pulmonary veins from your heart.
Managed to asphyxiate it. Not that it matters anymore. But before
they did this, your heart still looked like a heart. Today, I decided
to tear a piece of that muscle and, with an old silver chain that
I had in my possession, make a necklace. This way, to feel your
heart against mine. I don't think the others saw this. It is meant
to be a memento mori of you. Literally, to remember your death.
I also held your heart in my hand to see if it would miraculously
beat. It did not. I could not resuscitate it. The other killers look at
me strangely. I think that they realize that you are mine. So your
heart will always beat against mine.

Heart you,
Adrien

AN OLD DRY WIPE BOARD in the Emergency Room acted as a palimpsest, a blurred glimpse into the hospital's obscure history. In this board, one could observe the remnants of the word "critical" with its uncrossed t and misshapen a. There were lineages of other words that shed light into the presentations of the patients in the hospital. The residue of the words "sepsis," "pneumonia," and "myocardial infarction" all congealed together to brew a disease process singularly its own.

Today, the board revealed the presence of a "cutter" in the rear, left corridor of the ER. Upon starting her shift, Tess had immediately spied her in the ER corridor, on a gurney, and knew exactly what she must do. After she finished her duties in the hospital, Tess planned for another project. The cutter, a girl in her late teens, donned entirely in black, looked morose, not hysterical. Tess had seen them in this town, these Goths who dressed and acted this way. She knew what they must feel like, these black apparitions of the night who needed assurance despite feeling that they were somehow unable to be categorized. She felt for them like she would a dog that had been cut in the belly, writhing in pain. Though the girl would have liked to appear indifferent to the patients around her, she was now and then gazing around to view her audience. People were looking and a certain notoriety was being attached to her. Tess wanted this cutter as her patient and made a request to her senior resident, Abigail. Chaos was amok in the ER as gurneys were being set up in the corridors due to the shortage of rooms and the sheer abundance of the sick. The senior resident had no time tonight for teaching and didn't even wince at the request. Without close supervision, psychiatric cases were usually not reserved for medical students, but Abigail had unknowingly acquiesced.

After her night shift, Tess, too, would cut herself. Cut herself as deeply as would be necessary. This was work, her duty, and not some psychological experiment in which she had partaken. It was unfortunate that she was always one step behind her patients. It would be so wonderful if she anticipated their moves. They would be amazed that she was so knowledgeable about their illnesses, so compassionate toward them. Tess approached the cutter, a girl named Carissa. Attached to her torn, black shirt, a pin. "Carissa is weird," it said. As Tess had thought. Her intuitions were getting better with each patient.

The wound looked fresh, likely today's. Two inches spanning the entire length of her wrist. Superficial. No, Carissa hadn't meant to kill herself. This was pure performance, staged. Tess glimpsed another cut, smaller and older. It ran in the forearm. A dried-up red lake. Carissa would do this again. She would return for an encore to please her audience, now that she knew she had made a fan of Tess.

Without Anesthesia

Dear Tess,

I blew you up today. Again and again, in photographs. You became super life-sized. I tried to see what I couldn't when I was with you, dissecting you. Tried to see you in these mechanical reproductions, your body parts, blown up in images, and reproduced, again and again. As if you were hiding something from me that would come to light with the camera and film, the indexical image that would not lie, that would tell me who you really were. You were like Warhol's Marilyn to me. I replicated you, perhaps to numb those horrifying images of you, cut up and severed. To compulsively repeat the trauma. Again and again. As if I had missed the encounter with you. Already. Always, already missed it with you. Each shade of the photographs was lighter than the next. Your lips, a crimson blue, were slowly, repetitively, diluting themselves of your reality. The haze of your glassy pupils was losing that severed glimmer. Even in film, you were slowly disintegrating, removing yourself from me. I held on. Tightly. I knew that I could find you. Eventually. But, ultimately, it was of no use. I then decided to paste the best, most flattering pieces of your body parts into a collage of sorts. I must admit, it looked grotesque, the diminutive and the large images, the vivid and the pale, all congealed together with paste on cardboard. But this was really the best representation of you. The fucked-up reality that you had become. And the camera, the film, had conspired to create this real image of you. They alone told the truth that you had become. The others had already seen it. I wished to ignore it. You had become this. Completely fucked-up.

Again, so so sorry,
Adrien

ARCHIVED MEDICAL RECORDS

Name: Levkowitz, Allan
MR#: 246-74-8544
Huntington Memorial Hospital
Pasadena, California
June 27, 1972

History of Present Illness: This is a 49-year-old gentleman presenting today in the ER with having been physically and sexually assaulted by a group of men. By history, the episode occurred three days ago in West Hollywood when Mr. Levkowitz was "kicked at," "beat up," and "cursed at" (with derogatory, anti-homosexual slurs) while walking in, what is considered to be, a gay neighborhood. He was then sexually assaulted and battered when the group of men forcibly inserted a glass bottle into his rectum. The bottleneck subsequently broke within it. No history of head trauma or loss of consciousness is elicited. The patient states that he was "mortified" by this incident. He did not present to the hospital earlier because he was ashamed and embarrassed. No witnesses were identified to corroborate this event.

Social History: The patient is a bartender. He is single and lives in Los Angeles. Denies tobacco use. Drinks alcohol three times a week.

Family History: Adopted. No next of kin is reported.

Past Medical History: None

Medications: None

Review of Systems: Negative.

Vitals: T:98.1F P:90 R:12 BP:140/80

General: The patient is a well-nourished, well-developed gentleman who appears his stated age. A healed scar appears below his right eye. No evidence of external injury is present.

HEENT: No evidence of head trauma. Throat appears patent. Mallampati Grade III.

Heart: Regular rate and rhythm. II/VI systolic ejection murmur is auscultated in the lower left sternal border.

Lungs: Clear

Abdomen: Tender to palpation; No guarding or rigidity.

Lower extremities: No clubbing, cyanosis, or edema.

Rectal Examination: No evidence of perianal trauma.

Neurological: Alert and oriented to time, place, person, and situation. Abstraction intact. Cranial nerves II-XII intact. Pupils equal and reactive to light and accommodation (PERLA). Extraocular movements remain intact. No muscular deficits noted.

Labs: Complete Metabolic Panel is within normal limits

Plain X-Ray: Component of a glass bottle is present in the rectum

Assessment: This is an otherwise healthy 49-year old gentleman who was sexually battered three days ago. Plain X-ray reveals a shard of broken glass in his rectum.

Plan:

1. Perform endoscopy to remove bottle fragment

2. Discharge patient home if stable

John Wilson, M.D.

Emergency Department Physician

T.,

Today we colostomized you, punctured and cut your inside's insides, the intestines. The large and small next to one another. It looked like a large serpent circling a smaller one, ready to attack. But did you know that the smaller intestine is actually longer and more of a work horse than the larger one? Yours was about 20 feet long. I measured it. I'm detailing you, minutely, down to the tissues. Your juices flowed once we cut into the larger intestine. It smelled putrid. I almost gagged, but then remembered that it was you. I needed to breathe every ounce of you, feel you as my own, even if it meant that it would be unpleasant at times. Those killers, my bastardized blood brothers, had cut your small intestines and were lassoing it as if it were rope, tossing it around like sausage. You are mere meat to them. Something they cut and study. Something they can dispense. I'm afraid that they may even eat you one of these days, those fucking cannibals. Then I hear a disgusting shout from one of them as they cut into your rectum. "She's full of shit. She has shit in her rectum." I'm vehement, but remain silent throughout. I'm learning to control myself.

Still loyal,
Adrien

Tess,

You're barely alive now. You no longer look like your old self,
the self I knew so many months ago. You've been disemboweled,
unknowingly raped, your uterus hangs outside of your body, no
longer yours. They prod it, identifying this and that. They treat it
as a piece of meat, one that has been gnawed by a filthy, old black
cat that hasn't eaten in ages. It's a hysterectomy, what they did
to you. Did you know that, not so long ago, Charcot and Freud
thought that a hysterectomy would cure hysteria in young women,
a malady of the uterus? A young woman like you, in her early
20s. From the looks of it, you had problems before you came here.
When I first eyed you, you looked so pale and gaunt. I thought that
maybe no one had fed you in ages. I could see the little hook of your
ulnar bone jutting out. And then there were other signs. Your eyes
were overflowing their sockets. The ribs showed. Your chest caved
in. Yes, there were others in the room. But I knew you would be
ours. I had looked into those glassy eyes and you signaled back
with them in silence. It was then that I first glimpsed that small
tattoo of yours. Barely visible, at the nape, hidden by that matted
hair. *Tess.* All in cursive, but small. I had thought of Tess of the
d'Urbervilles, raped.

Sorry,
Adrien

Dear Tess (I'm not sure anymore),

Before the ink has had a chance to dry, the page turns on you and me. It tries to create a story, a telos, for us, but it literally turns me against you. When I'm writing these letters, I am looking elsewhere. Not at you. I'm thinking of a terrible tale, a fantastic nightmare, which plagued you, but who is to say that it's correct? It is my hand that directs me to write and this ink that flows from my pen. It is the betrayer. The tattooed inscription of your name on your neck bothers me. It is again the ink and, more or less, it's permanent. It reads: *Tess.* And cursive at that. Not very clean. Not neatly juxtaposed. The letters at once too close to one another and the T a little far apart. You had done this fast, too fast, at a tattoo parlor, unhygienic in its practices, needle dipped into ink, tainted with others' blood and fluids, not your type of place, catering to scum, but you had to get a message across, a message that you were probably ashamed to divulge completely, so you hid it behind your long, glorious hair, at your nape. An act of rebellion. But can I be sure that Tess is even your real name? Or, if the tattoo names another? A secret lover, perhaps? Someone whom you had hoped to become? These letters reproduce themselves infinitely. They make me question why you have been thrust upon me. To open you. Completely. To read you. As text. But your organs connote different things, infinitely point to other references, all of whose strings I cannot possibly follow.

Forever lost,
A.

TESS NOW LIVES in an apartment, alone. It's in a sleazy part of town. Her neighbors are meth addicts. She knows this. She also knows that she's very alone. It's a new town. She doesn't know anyone. She misses home, but knows that she can't go back. Can't return as she was before. Changes. She was never good with changes. She looks herself in the cracked mirror. She doesn't recognize herself. The new haircut. Makeup that looks disastrous. She makes a mental note to work on this. She needs to work on a lot of things. This will take some time. The blades from the hospital. She takes one in her right hand, between thumb and forefinger. 2 cm., like the cut she'll make. She hasn't cut herself before. Remember: superficial, not deep. The blade glides smoothly across her wrist. Very easy. She feels pain but also excitement. Endorphins escape and trigger her heart and brain. There's blood. There's pain. For the moment, she forgets her real problems. She thinks of Carissa, of how she felt. Tess has mistaken. Her intuitions are still not so good. Carissa didn't perform. This is real. Tess is bleeding a bit more. But the pain sears through. It digs deeper. It's relentless. A rush of blood to the head leads her outside to the sunken and dirty snow that composes this town and makes Tess feel just as dirty inside, the way she always feels but feels more each day, and more so with the way she looks right now, with her new haircut and makeup that the stylist, she is sure, had mocked, and the blood trickles from her wrist, falling and covering the dirty snow as she remembers back to another bloodstained snow, so long ago, but she is so far now as the pain bites her back hard and she doesn't have time to react.

Dear Tess,

These letters will find their way to you. Someday. I'm sure of it,
just as I'm sure of my love for you. Don't get me wrong. These are
not love letters. These are lettres mortes. Letters to commemorate
your death. But don't misunderstand me, either. This is not dead
letter mail: mail that cannot be delivered to the addressee nor
returned to sender. Nor letters that can be opened despite being
private, so as to offer clues to origin and destination. These are
not those types of letters, Tess. I know where you are and where
you will be. I can address these letters to you. They may take
some time getting there, but they will find you. But don't you
see? In some way, you are my dead letter mail as I open and try
to read you and find clues. Where did you originate? And where
were you destined? Who addressed you? And were you stamped
with appropriate postage? I think: what if I never opened you?
Would you be in a dead letter office somewhere, being burned and
destroyed? I'm so sorry, dear. Your fate is much worse. You found
your way to the charnel house instead and are being tortured
here.

Your fateful postman,
Adrien

Archived Medical Records

Name: Malinowski, Arthur
MR# 367-80-9454
Los Angeles County Hospital
Los Angeles, CA
July 17, 1987

History of Present Illness: This is a 66-year old gentleman, without a significant past medical history, who presents today with several episodes of "jerking" of his arms and legs. The patient states that he was unconscious during these unwitnessed events and only remembers waking up disoriented and lethargic. Prior to these episodes, he was watching a show on television with "a lot of flashing and flickering lights." He reports urinary incontinence and tongue lacerations. Per history, he appears to have been postictal for 1 hour before he regained a normal level of consciousness. The patient denies using any new medications. He denies a history of substance use, particularly cocaine. There does not appear to have been any antecedent parasitic or viral infections, history of head trauma, or sleep deprivation. The patient does not report any recent travel, contact with pets, or recently eating undercooked pork.
Social History: The patient is a retired cook. He is a widow and lives in Los Angeles. Denies smoking or using other substances. Drinks two glasses of red wine per week.
Family History: Adopted. No next of kin reported.
Review of Systems: As above.
Vitals: T: 97.7 F P: 98 R: 12 BP: 130/80
General: The patient is a well-nourished, well-developed gentleman who appears younger than his stated age. He is neatly groomed. A healed scar appears below his right eye.
HEENT: No evidence of head trauma. A tongue laceration with minor bleeding is present. Throat appears patent. Mallampati Grade III.
Heart: Regular rate and rhythm. II/VI systolic ejection murmur is auscultated in the lower left sternal border.

Lungs: Clear to auscultation bilaterally
Abdomen: Benign.
Lower extremities: No clubbing, cyanosis, or edema.
Neurological: Alert and oriented to time, place, person, and situation. Good fund of knowledge. Abstract abilities remain intact. Cranial nerves II-XII intact. Pupils equal and reactive to light and accommodation (PERLA). No nystagmus is present. Extraocular movements remain intact. Muscular strength in the lower and upper extremities 5/5 bilaterally. Deep-tendon reflexes—biceps 2/4, triceps ¼, patellar 2/4, Achilles 2/4 (bilaterally). Bilateral plantar flexor responses. Negative Romberg Test. Finger to nose reveals no dysmetria or dystaxia.

Assessment:
1. New onset generalized tonic-clonic seizures in an elderly gentleman without a significant past medical history or provoking factors. Possibly, photosensitive epilepsy, although this is unusual given the patient's age and the low incidence of this type of epilepsy.

Plan:
   1. Admit to the Neurology ward. Rule out neoplasm and an infectious process: A) Brain MRI with and without contrast, B) EEG, C) Complete blood count and metabolic panel, D) Urinary toxicology screen, E) Lumbar puncture, F) Blood and urine cultures, G) Seizure precautions
   2. Pureed diet; Aspiration precautions
   3. Physical therapy consult
   4. Social services consult

Stanley Brown, M.D., Ph.D.
Attending, Dept. of Internal Medicine

Without Anesthesia

Poor Tess,

The decapitation began today. We had exhausted the rest of your
tattered body and organs, so it was expected. I say expected, but
nothing is ever so, is it? I'm sure that you were not expected to
die and suffer this bitter torment. In your case, the letter arrived
at its (unexpected) destination a little too early and it was torn
and shred in pieces. We shred it more. I cannot glue the pieces
together and read the message, if there ever was one. You remain
so enigmatic to me, you poor, young soul. I try to read your history
from the face alone. Your nose is sloped, beautiful angle and
profile. Your eyes are now too glassy, but they conceal a vibrant
pupil and apertures that once filtered light so perfectly that
you could see through the hypocrisy that fucks everything up.
There's a symmetrical dimple in your chin that makes you look
handsome, somewhat androgynous. You were a beautiful young
woman and look what's happened to you now. But hold on. The
sawing is almost done now. The others did most of the work and I
merely watched (is the witness guilty, too?). They struggled. They
cursed. And, then, unexpectedly, the head was cleaved from your
body. You, my dear, were decapitated. Severed.

So, so, sorry,
Adrien

ZAMORANO MADE HIS ENTRANCE into the Emergency Department dramatically with an uneven gait, using a tattered cane, indicating that this apparatus was part of him now. These two together, this was the old man. Despite this awkwardness, he ambulated with a purpose that the cane directed, his chest heaving, breathless. Making his way to the clerk, his breathing became shallower, faster, more ominous. He couldn't breathe, he said. The nurse quickly whisked him away. No time to inquire about his history. He was diaphoretic, tachypneic, hyperventilating. Signs that couldn't be ignored. A portable chest x-ray, stat. Pulmonary embolism, myocardial infarction, pneumothorax, all potential diagnoses. For this man, all potential deaths. A hypolucency in the x-ray film. A pneumothorax. Escaped air into the cavity and a collapse of the lungs. The physician directed the placement of a chest tube. The old man reached in his pocket for the dirty dagger and placed it in his left hand, forming a fist. The dagger had been a part of him far longer than the cane. It had a history encapsulated in dry, crusted blood. An inscription on its corrugated handle. "For A," it read. He felt the depths and ridges of the A and smiled, although he was still not breathing so well.

Tess,

They call you fucking stupid. I don't even listen to them anymore.
You can tell by the size of her brain, they say, so small. Her sulci
and gyri are too widely spaced apart. And they're smooth. I don't
listen anymore. I don't. They say that your brain is also fucked,
like the rest of you. Tess, did you have problems memorizing your
bible verses or your dramatic monologues? Were you religious or a
hedonist? I touch your brain as we separate the three layers from
one another. The first to go is the dura mater. Tough mother in
Latin. And speaking of mothers, was yours abusive or nurturing?
I think kind. You look too wholesome to be brought up in an
abusive household. The second layer, the arachnoid. Spider. Did
you, too, weave webs like Penelope to ward off her suitors until
Odysseus arrived from battle? Were you ever in love? Yes, I want
to know all these things, but I can't. You came anonymously to
us and it's our job to learn your body as if it were our own. But we
can never really learn you, can we? Your soul is out of reach. You
have woven webs for us and it leads us nowhere. The pia mater, the
softest of the three, is the last to go. It encloses the brain as if it
were one with it. So close to it, but a different substance altogether.
This is my relationship to you. I feel you, feel that I am you, but I'm
not. We probably come from different places. But I feel that I know
you. That you and I are the pia mater and the brain. I know that
you were smart. You are my brainy.

Forever, your pia,
Adrien

TESS HAD ASKED TO SEE HIM in the ward once he had stabilized. She had spent the entire night in the ER with the old man and wanted to see his progress. It had been a long night, but also educational. The old man called himself Zamorano and verbally enunciated each letter as if he were to embark on an etymological lesson. It appeared that he wanted others to believe that he was the last of the Roma, emphasizing this through his accent, mannerisms, and clothes. Although he was now donned in the generically faded green hospital attire, he had worn a paisley dress shirt that, although threadbare, looked regal. He looked the part of a king who had been ostracized from his community and magically transported to the present time. For a man of his age, he had abundant hair, but of a complete gray that could be mistaken for a whiter shade of white if one were asked to identify it on a color palette. It suited him. He had sideburns. He had worn a scarf around his neck. Yet another sign that he was somehow someone more than his present circumstances allowed. From another perspective, however, it all looked feigned. She thought about these two contradictory notions, but the images were too much, too fast for a sustained reflection.

Tess had initially seen the old man in the ER when the chest tube had been placed into the space between the linings of his left lung. He had been sedated and she had had the opportunity to examine him thoroughly, as was expected of a medical student. In palpating his abdomen, she had noticed a plastic bag with a collection of feces. She had read about these colostomies in medical school, but, in viewing it, she couldn't conceal her utter disgust. To her, human excrement was personal, and to see Zamorano's waste displayed on him so brazenly sickened her. She also thought that she had seen engorged veins through his abdomen, the so called "caput medusae" sign of alcoholic disease, but she wasn't sure.

She immediately knew, however, that Zamorano would be her intrepid teacher, that her future would be somehow linked to his. She knew that she wanted to feel everything that this man was experiencing, everything that he had had experienced. History was inscribed within him. History was he. He was a plethora of illness, abundance of knowledge, and, at that moment, the goal for which she had toiled became vividly clear as if she were receiving divine visions like Juliana of Norwich had. She saw herself as martyr, as giver of hope to her patients. No experience would be taken from her, no illness barred from her. This Zamorano, he was her teacher now. And she would be an astute follower, a devout worshiper. She vowed to experience him, learn him, breathe him, until she was history herself.

The old man and Tess now eyed one another. His sudden gaze startled her, as if she were caught glimpsing a secret that was not meant for her. They looked one another piercingly for mere seconds, although to Tess it seemed like hours. She had seen these eyes before, in another time and place, on another being, and it shocked her that they should find themselves on the face of this man, now. Then he turned away as if he were bored of her, bored of this room and encounter. She came up to him. "Mr. Zamorano, good morning, my name is Tess, the medical student from last night. I'm not sure if you remember me."

Silence. Then sudden laughter. It jolted Tess.

"Of course I do, young lady, do you take me for an old fool? I may look the part, but I am the wiser."

"Certainly, that's not what I meant, Mr. Zamorano. It's just that you were so sick last night and you may have not recognized certain things. I didn't mean to imply anything by that. Please excuse me."

"You need not apologize, dear lady Tess, you certainly have been a dear host to me already. I know that you were up with me late last night before they took me up here, in this room. You have very kind eyes and kind words to match."

In mentioning the eyes, Zamorano caught Tess again as if she were a voyeur, glimpsing a part of him that was very private, very dangerous.

Tess changed subjects and asked about his health. How was he doing? Was he breathing easier? The chest tube looked well placed, she said, the secretions looked normal. He would be feeling better in no time if he just rested. She would be by to see him later in the evening.

Brainy,

We are dissecting the lobes of your brain slowly. It is such a daunting project. And we don't have much time. We have already rid you of your body. You'd be pleased to know that you are finally rid of yourself. And this is a good thing. Trust me. Your body's odor, even with the formaldehyde, was making me so nauseous that I could barely come back and visit it. The others gave me looks. What do you want with her? Is she your girlfriend? Girlfriend in a perpetual coma? And their boisterous and cynical laughter would be too much for me. At these times, a glimmer of water would suggest itself from my eyes and then I knew it was time to leave. They could not see my crying. These fluids were too personal and only reserved for you, my brainy. But then, I saw and couldn't control myself. The temporal lobe of the left side of your brain was contused. Bruised. Speckles of blood surrounded it. Accidental? Intentional? Initially, I imagine a motor vehicle accident. You are drunk or sleepy, and your car rolls over and the force of the blow impacts your brain. But, then, the image of the mother returns. This time, she is hard. Hard as concrete. She abuses you and batters you with a blunt object. Why? Because your father is in love with you and not with her. And this is too much for her. She has seen him caressing you, the object of his affection. It's the return of the Electra complex and your mother feels excluded from this equation. She is tough and unyielding. And there is yet another possibility. You, walking alone from school, clutching your handbag in the darkened corridors of an alley when a thief, who is waiting furtively for you, bludgeons you with a rock, grabs your bag and runs. So many possibilities for you and yet you are always victim, never transgressor. I can't continue anymore today. That blow is too hard on me.

Adrien

T.,

I cut out your face today. Like some form of childhood project,
I cut around the demarcated Magic-Marker lines. I was never
good at that, coloring and cutting within the margins. A part of
your lip slipped away from the cut. Pardon me. Your face was of
no use to them, except the eyes and ears, which they took like
some greedy bastards. I'll get those back. Trust me. Your face felt
like papier-mache, a bundle of papers that were glued together
to construct some sort of identity for you. It felt like it would slip
to the floor and fall apart. It didn't. How fragile you are, though.
Without the bones to bolster it, your face felt so delicate. I made
out the outlines of your eyes, nose, and mouth. So very soft, all of
it. I imagined wearing your face like a mask during Carnevale,
masquerading as you. I'm planning to make a mold of it and have
your face in possession at all times. I can hear your objections
already. No, don't worry, Tess. It will be put to good use. I promise.
I won't let them fuck you up any more.

Always,
Adrien

SHE HAD THOUGHT ABOUT IT ALL NIGHT in the ER, caring for Zamorano among the gurneys, bags of IV fluid, syringes, and the impersonal nurses and doctors. No one truly cared whether Zamorano lived or died. It was true. He was another statistic, someone to be efficiently dispensed of, for the good, one hoped, but his death was just that. A death and nothing more. His life amounted to the same. Tissue and fluid to be disposed of as efficiently as possible. In memory, she glimpsed the bucket of dead tissue of her gross anatomy days. Meat. It was all rotten meat. Tears swelled in her eyes, but she tricked herself into thinking about something else so as to distract herself. She knew that she would shoulder this blatant disdain, and care for every individual as if her life depended on it. She, alone, would take on this responsibility.

But her thoughts segued into the practicality of the matter, into the practicality of the disease that had been thrust upon her. She needed to refresh her memory. Zamorano's was the first clinical case of a pneumothorax that she had encountered. And it was in pathology, in her first-year of medical school, that she had first learned about this disease process. A pocket of air between the two layers of pleura. Collapse of the lungs. She knew how she would do this. No one would suspect it. All she needed was a syringe, a hygienic syringe filled with nothing but air.

Dearest Tess,

I returned from the graveyard just minutes ago. I was trying to
find you a permanent home here in Valhalla, New York. At Kensico
Cemetery. It's befitting you, this Valhalla, the hall of the slain in
Norse mythology, welcoming its heroes who died in combat. I was
trying to find your organs a place of repose here, not that filthy
lab where your tissues commingle with the dirt of the floor and
the vermin that feed upon it. I carried your left arm and hand as
well as the remains of your face. I decided on the nose and ears,
for convenience, which I placed in a clean Zip-Loc bag. I had read
about the "maschalismos" ritual, performed to prevent the dead
from taking revenge on her killers. Although I knew that you
would never do me harm, I still needed some assurance. You can
do what you want with the others. I strung your parts along a
cord and passed it under my armpit. The ritual demanded it. Oh,
Tess! Have you heard of anything more horrible, my dear? I am
beyond forgiveness. Once the ritual had been performed, I dug a
small grave, 2 feet deep, and carefully placed your remains there.
I plan to make this grave deeper and more hospitable for you, at
6 feet, as I dispense more organs. The rest don't know about my
undertaking. To not arouse suspicion, it has to be only one organ
a time. Those organs that they have studied well and do not need
anymore. In this cemetery, I plan to resurrect and make you new
again.

Forever, your Odin,
Adrien

Bismarck, North Dakota. Winter. 1981. Snow laden with filth, decorated with fresh wolf's blood. The wolf that Adrien's father has just slaughtered with a shotgun. Adrien, age nine, weeps horribly, wishing that maybe ten would be different, that he would be braver. The cries of the wolf reverberate in Adrien's mind. The speckle of dirt that leaps from nowhere, the wolf. With wolf in mid-air, Adrien imagines the texture of the skin. Tough, hard, abrasive, homeless. In an instant, the shot. Father is always so proud, always ready with his pistol. He hears the growl, turns around, and shoots. So quick for his father, so slow for Adrien. The boy's first hunting expedition, his first remembrance of tears. Wolf in mid-air, trying to make a living, trying to survive. Slaughtered before being given the chance to show his skills. Adrien sees himself hurling in midair. He is wolf. Running for the dead wolf, Adrien slips. Father runs after him. Adrien reaches the dead wolf and holds it. Hands sticky with hardened, red blood. So very red, so very dirty. Adrien cries uncontrollably now. Be a man, boy, father says. A fucking man. Adrien holds the wolf closely, the skin rough but safe. Father, sickened, severs the union. A blow to the cheeks from father. Adrien feels it completely and smiles.

Archived Medical Records

Bukowsky, Arnold
MR# 504-97-2146
Memorial Medical Center
Ashland, WI
July 3, 1996

History of Present Illness: This is a 68-year old right-handed gentleman, with a history of a previous colostomy, who presents today with acute right-sided weakness and an inability to talk. The patient noticed garbled speech and dysarthria at approximately 2:30 pm while talking on the telephone. Soon thereafter, he noticed weakness on the right side of his body and fell to the ground. The patient dialed 911 and was emergently transported to the ER via ambulance. During transit, the patient lost his ability to vocalize words. No other history can be related as the patient lives alone and the event was not witnessed.

SH: Lives alone. No next of kin.

FH: Unable to be obtained as patient appears to be mute.

ROS: Unable to be ascertained. See above for history.

PE: V: 97.8F P:102 R:18 BP:130/75

General: Patient is a well-nourished, well-developed elderly gentleman who appears his stated age. He is well groomed; an old scar appears below his right eye.
HEENT: Patent pharynx. Mallampati Grade III.
Heart: Regular rate and rhythm. II/VI systolic ejection murmur is auscultated in the lower left sternal border.
Lungs: Clear to auscultation bilaterally.
Abdomen: Empty colostomy pouch present. No signs of infection around the stoma.

Lower extremities: No clubbing, cyanosis, or edema.
Neurological: Patient is alert and appears cognizant of his environment. Cannot assess orientation, as patient is globally aphasic. Cranial nerves II-XII intact. Pupils equal and reactive to light and accommodation (PERLA). No nystagmus is present. Extraocular movements remain intact. Left upper and lower extremities 5/5, bilaterally. Right upper and lower extremities 3/5, bilaterally. Deep-tendon reflexes—biceps 1/4, triceps 2/4, patellar 2/4, Achilles 2/4 (bilaterally). Bilateral plantar flexor responses. The patient cannot follow directions to assess for dysmetria.
NIH Stroke Scale (NIHSS)=18

Assessment and Plan:

1. Acute onset of global aphasia and right-sided weakness in an otherwise healthy 68-year old gentleman. Patient's clinical signs (DTRs and plantar flexor response on the right) do not correspond to what appears to be a left middle cerebral artery stroke. However, the patient is a t-PA candidate as onset of symptoms < 3 hours, brain CT is without hemorrhage, and complete metabolic panel is within normal limits. IV t-PA to be administered 0.9 mg/kg, infused over 60 minutes with 10% of the total dose administered as an initial intravenous bolus over 1 minute. DO NOT exceed 90 mg total. Labetalol 20 mg IV, slow infusion, to be given if systolic BP > 190 mm Hg and diastolic >110 mm Hg. NPO. No punctures for the first 24 hours. No anti-platelet agents to be administered. The patient is to be transferred to the Neuro ICU with orders according to the acute stroke protocol. Diffusion-weighted MRI of the brain is to be performed after the patient is stabilized.

Rajeev Singh, M.D.
Department of Neurology

THE NEEDLE FELT a little sharp at first. Bevel up, she had inserted it into her left chest cavity. She didn't know why she had inserted it into the left. Not that it mattered anyway. Perhaps it was because of the lessons that had been thrust upon her in her childhood years when writing with her left hand was criticized, even condemned by her parents. She knew that she was born left-handed but, somehow, in some manner, through indoctrination perhaps, she had emerged right-handed. As she was pushing the syringe into her chest, she lucidly saw the thousands of lines on hundreds of papers that she had inscribed as a child, "I am right-handed, I am right-handed, I am right-handed..." It had seemed to her that this torture would never end, but just as she were about to give up, she had written her last sentence. She didn't know if she were unconsciously creating the pneumothorax in the left lung due to a vendetta she had harbored against her left hand for making part of her childhood so miserable. She quickly dismissed the idea. She had more important matters to which to attend.

It took a while for her to feel anything at all. But, suddenly, she did. A little discomfort in her left chest. Tightness. She had difficulty inhaling. What she had taken for granted was suddenly out of her control. Zamorano emerged in her thoughts. She was doing this all for him. For him, but also for her patients. She must not forget her plan, her vision.

She was sparing of the air. Deliberating between a pneumothorax that would seriously harm and gain her admission to the hospital and one that would resolve itself, she opted for the latter. The former would raise suspicion, lend itself to speculation. She was smarter. She still needed to learn. And a hospital stay would be a setback, in all respects. She still needed to observe Zamorano and learn from him. She was still not breathing so well, and felt a little closer to Zamorano. She should be closer still. She justified her actions in this manner. She would let the pneumothorax resolve itself, now that she knew the tinge of what Zamorano had experienced. It was the best that could be done under the circumstances.

Adrien had imagined the meeting just like this. The desk separating them, the clinical chair waiting for him, the calm timbre of the doctor's voice. It was always the same setting, mannerisms, and dialogue. Adrien needed comfort. He needed sweating hands to tell him that someone cared. The doctor's voice was so far off, a voice that reverberated and hinted of shame, gesturing that Adrien was somehow abnormal. The doctor, graying at the temples but probably not yet middle-aged, advocated "real life experience" for Adrien if he were to undergo surgery. Without this experience, the doctor could not recommend and would not undertake it. Adrien had heard this before, but thought that perhaps this doctor would be different. He would find another doctor. He would succeed with his plan, one way or another. He hadn't even broached the topic of the face with the doctor.

THE FOLLOWING EVENING, Tess was still experiencing shortness of breath when she entered the ER. She was breathing a little faster, but it wasn't noticeable. Certainly not to Abigail who was always running around, doing this or that, cleaning up the loose ends of the admissions that somehow managed to linger around in the morning. Abigail was the model for what a senior resident hoped to become, what she hoped to achieve. Her hair in a ponytail, she was efficient, quick, and matter-of-fact. A certain aura attached to her. She appeared as she was. An open book with sentences constructed simply, meaning what they meant. Abigail had no time to explore the hidden meaning of things, the connotations that cling and make meaning so much more complicated.

In a way, Tess envied her. Envied that simplicity that made life appear so easy, so fluid as if it were running itself, a perfect machinery that would never derail. By comparison, Tess thought about her life. How utterly messy it was. As if words were more than enough and somehow never sufficient. Meaning that would multiply itself and produce intentions that were never meant in the first place. And especially now. She had moved into this new town and was already reading so much into it. How were people perceiving her? Did her haircut look too obvious? Was she believable? Could she really hope to encapsulate the myriad disease processes that plagued those whom she encountered? She was always thinking, thinking about her next move, and, now, even anticipating the actions of her patients. She really was becoming exhausted, both emotionally and physically.

The paragon of efficiency, Abigail glimpsed Tess, albeit for a few seconds, and scurried towards her. "And how are you, Tess? Hope it won't be a rough night like a couple of nights ago. Zamorano really did me in. Placing that chest tube wasn't easy. And the arterial line. That was even harder."

Tess wasn't used to Abigail complaining. It caught her off-guard. But Abigail had a sharp memory. Remembering the patients' names as if her life depended on it. No other person, be it the Attending or another resident, was so collective, so sharp. She recollected lab values, vitals, and family histories unlike any other. A scientific notebook, a ledger, whose pages would never be deleted. But the complaining. Tess wasn't used to this.

"I'm alright. Thanks for asking. That was a rough night for me as well. I watched Zamorano that entire night. Really learned a lot from his case. I studied up on the various pneumothoraces and pleural effusions this entire week. Really interesting stuff."

Tess didn't want to appear like a sycophant, like so many medical students did. She couldn't stand it. But she also enjoyed Abigail's demeanor and her concern for the medical students. She wanted to appear somewhat enthusiastic, to indirectly thank her for the time she spent teaching them when time permitted.

"I'm glad you thought that. I've been watching you interact with the patients and you're doing a good job. You take it pretty seriously, like I did. I think you've got a good future ahead of you. Strong work."

She remembered this phrase from her first day in the ER, overhearing an Attending remark it to another resident. She had thought it odd and still did. Why not "good work" or "excellent work"? She thought about the sexist implications of "strong." But she really didn't want to explore that aspect of things. Not today. She wanted to be pulled away from all that and follow the tracks that Abigail herself was marking.

Adrien was reminiscing about a past that may have not existed. He couldn't tell for sure. His parents clung to and created a static bubble around him. He was perhaps five, maybe six. He knew at that time that these were the only parents he ever wanted. He couldn't imagine life without them. He knew of death and the possibility that they could be taken away from him. He would die and go with them. When they left home for work, he sobbed and screamed so outrageously that his nanny, Elisabetta, an import from Italy, would yell, Basta, Basta, over and over again. He hated her, blamed her for their departures. Elisabetta had a particular mole. A blend of hues of vanilla and chocolate so that it looked almost creamy, shaped like a star. He wanted to associate this mole with a black hole into which he was thrust. Except the mole wasn't black. He wanted to hate this mole as much as he did Elisabetta. But this star shined back at him, gave him hope that they would return. No, he loved this star. Couldn't imagine life without it. Every time that he glanced at it.

The aseptic syringe. Tess holds it like a pencil. But this is no writing. She is not used to this. The process is so new to her. She contemplates its consequences. For a moment only. And then she shoots it. In the arm. A chemical derivative from that which has made her who she is. Crack wars. Within herself. These chemicals, will her body reject them? Please don't. Please don't. I'm too far now. I can't remember my way back. Three months now. Her brown hair, lank, with bangs. The hairstylist had recommended the style. Not too severe, reasonable for now, when she was just starting out. The stylist had smiled, but she wasn't sure whether she was being mocked or if this were her friendly manner. She was too far now. Her bodily angles were slowly changing. Would they notice? She had never liked them. Changes. But she had no choice. The syringe had delivered the substance. Twice weekly, three months. A new hairstyle. New clothes. She is to start a new medical school. Only a few months now, a new life. She was too far now.

Adrien lies in the gurney, cold. There is no one to help him through this process. This is the last of the microsurgeries, the most complicated. He is to be wheeled into the operating room shortly. The arterial line has been placed. Momentarily, the anesthesia will be infused. Night and day, he has been thinking of Tess, of the cadaverous mess of a body that has been thrust upon him, of hope that she will be restored as she once was. He cannot turn back now.

Soon, the propofol will lull him into a transient death. He will be reborn, he thinks, when he awakens. Count down from 10, the anesthesiologist's calm voice resonates. 10, 9,8, 7, 6, 5… At 4, Tess seductively appears, bathed in light, her faced covered in a golden wire mesh jousting veil. She unveils. She is brutally disfigured. Her vulvar lips attached to her mouth. An enucleated eye. Scars cover her face. A big X. Teeth, blackened and separated. A horrific gap. She's a fucking mess. He can't believe what the Lord has sent him. She is dancing like an epileptic under attack. Saint Vitus's dance. She motions him to dance with her. The first dance with his new bride, before he goes under. She slithers toward him, her face contorted, her limbs choreoathetotic… 1.

Without Anesthesia

Archived Medical Records

Name: Madorsky, Leopold
MR#: 215-78-8050
Bergan Mercy Medical Center
Omaha, Nebraska
July 20, 1990

History of Present Illness: This is a 68-year old gentleman, without a significant past medical history, transported by the EMT unit after a stab to the abdomen. The patient was lying in an alley when passersby found him. The presumed stabbing was not witnessed, nor have any assailants been identified. As reported by the EMT unit, the patient was able to provide his name and a brief recount of events. In transit, the patient was found to be hypotensive and tachycardic. Time between initial assessment and transport is estimated to be approximately 30 minutes. No other history can be obtained.
Vitals: BP: 90/60 P: 120 T: 99.4F R: 22

General: Patient is alert and oriented to person, place, and situation. He is able to provide the current year, but neither the month nor date. Appears disheveled and unkempt. Stated age appears accurate.
HEENT: No evidence of head trauma or lacerations. Throat appears patent. Mallampati Grade III.
Heart: Regular rate and rhythm. II/VI systolic ejection murmur is heard in the lower left sternal border.
Lungs: Clear to auscultation bilaterally
Abdomen: Stab wound to the left lower quadrant, appearing relatively clean. Positive bowel sounds. No rebound tenderness. Slight guarding.
Lower extremities: No clubbing, cyanosis, or edema.

47.

Neurological: Good fund of knowledge. Abstract abilities remain intact. Cranial nerves II-XII intact. Pupils equal and reactive to light and accommodation (PERLA). No nystagmus present. Extraocular movements remain intact. Muscular strength in the lower and upper extremities appears intact. Bilateral plantar flexor responses.

Assessment/Plan:

A 68-year old gentleman with a stab to the abdomen and associated hypotension and tachycardia.

Plan:

Admit to the ICU for continued resuscitation and restoration of physiologic homeostasis.

1. Hemoglobin and Hematocrit levels. Complete Metabolic Panel. PT, PTT, INR. Type and cross 4 units of blood and then transfuse.

2. Normal saline: 1 Liter bolus and then continue with 150 cc/hr.

3. Gram negative coverage (Enterococcus) with ampicillin/sulbactam until cultures return.

4. CT of abdomen without contrast.

5. Surgical consult. Possible need of diverting colostomy. Will await surgical team's recommendations.

6. NPO.

Matthew Heines, M.D.
Intensivist

Dear Tess,

I am still reeling from that blow. It caught me so unexpectedly. I
had never thought about what had killed you, but now I imagine
these possibilities. Some are ridiculous, I know. But some have
their merits. The blow is all that I have to go by. There are no
other remnants of your wasted body that can offer me more
clues. Perhaps you were an epileptic and, during an attack, you
battered your head. Or a narcoleptic with sleep attacks and
cataplexy who fell everywhere, was bruised everywhere. Do you
remember, your heart was small? Recurrent syncopal attacks
could have devastated you and traumatized your body and brain.
Perhaps. I'm not sure anymore. The explanation for your death is
probably both profound and simple. You could have been prone to
depression and suicidal ideations and caused the blow yourself.
The list can go on. Please, Tess, offer me more clues to go by.

Need help,
Adrien

A FORTNIGHT HAD PASSED since Zamorano entered the hospital. He was ensconced in a corner room at his request. Strangely, although he had been recovering quite well until late, his health had recently taken an unexpected deterioration. A fever was brewing and its source had yet to be discovered. Laboratory tests had not detected much. Chest x-rays and CT scans had also been of no help. More tests were to be ordered.

Tess noticed that Zamorano requested darkness and had done so since he arrived in this room. The first night that she had spent with him in the ER seemed so long ago, although it had been just a few weeks. She could still breathe the darkness that enveloped them that night, as well as that peculiar smell which permeated the old man's body. She was used to peculiar and offensive odors that she encountered daily in the hospital, but Zamorano's was distinct and she couldn't quite discern its origin. It reminded her of an old church that she had once visited in Rome, at once familiar and old. She envisioned the beautifully crafted frescoes that she had seen there and recalled the odor that permeated the entire place. She had liked the experience and now realized that she did not dislike his odor either. She had wanted to ask Zamorano about his origins, but was always intimidated by his presence and her appearing to be too probing. She would ask him one day.

Her stomach was still recovering from the mouthwash poisoning that she had attempted after she had seen a six-year old boy overdose on Listerine. Who would've thought that she would swallow mouthwash one day just to feel her bodily reaction to it and empathize with this little boy? She had felt a bit ataxic and nauseous, but did not go far enough to use the activated charcoal that she had brought home from the ER. Her cautiousness still troubled her. She thought that this was just the beginning of what would happen to her body. It was being morphed every day and it would soon be shaped into what she envisioned since her first days in medical school. Her goal would soon be realized.

She was thinking such thoughts as she quickly knocked and entered

Zamorano's room. The room had grown darker and Zamorano's odor now was completely overpowering. Even the septic smell of the hospital was no match for that old, yet familiar, fragrance. Tess wondered if he were asleep. But his eyes opened quickly and, like so many instances before, she averted her gaze for a second before looking back at him.

"My lady Tess," he remarked raspily, "such joy today your presence brings. Please stay awhile." Tess had always noticed Zamorano's awkward sentence structures, but today this disparity seemed even more pronounced. She had attributed this to his ethnic, possibly Roma, origins and never thought about it too much. But perhaps because his voice seemed more hoarse than usual, the incongruity was markedly more noticeable.

"Of course, Mr. Zamorano. Although I still have patients to attend to in the ER. I'm very sorry if I woke you. I just wanted to pay you a visit."

"Nonsense, Lady Tess. I do not sleep any more. Everything is light around me, though my heart is dark. I feel unwell. Do you know how to cure me?"

Zamorano's plea was too abrupt for what Tess had anticipated. She hadn't seen him in this state before, and was a bit puzzled and moved by his strange allusions. She, however, responded immediately, unconsciously, automatically: " Oh, Mr. Zamorano. Of course, we'll cure you. We have the best doctors and residents here. One of us will find an answer, I'm sure."

"How do I feel, Lady Tess? You cannot possibly know. I'm miserable with this sickness."

It was as if someone had knifed her. Tess froze. Had she heard right? "You cannot possibly know" reverberated in her head like a bad echo from a nightmare. The force of Zamorano's statement was so powerful that she could not respond. Her thoughts were elsewhere now. But her tears had spoken when she couldn't. It was slow at first, the velocity of the tears, but they quickly gained momentum.

It was Zamorano who took notice now. He had not expected what he had just observed. No one had ever cried for him, so genuinely, so instantaneously. He gripped his small dagger, which he had concealed so well in his underpants, a little more forcefully now, as if not to be overcome by this girl's outpouring.

Regimen after surgery:

Month 1: Begin twice-monthly injections of 20 mg estradiol valerate or 2 mg estradiol cypionate. Also, take 1-2 mg/day sl (sublingual)-oral estradiol or 2-3 mg/day sl-oral estradiol valerate or a single 0.05 mg transdermal estradiol film changed weekly to prevent «bottoming out» of the serum estradiol level. If these injectibles are not available, employ a single 0.1mg transdermal estradiol film changed twice weekly, or 4 mg/day sl-oral estradiol, or 6 mg/day sl-oral estradiol valerate. Divide sl-oral doses into 2 takings per day (as for all the following oral drugs).

Month 2: Given continued health, add anti-androgens: 100 mg/day spironolactone plus fractional tablet (0.05-0.5 mg)/day finasteride. If spironolactone is not available but cyproterone acetate is, employ 10 mg/day cyproterone acetate. (Actually, a GnRH agonist is much more effective to reduce androgens and their effects, but it is also prohibitively expensive.)

Month 3: Given continued health, add progesterone or progestin: 200 mg/day oral progesterone, or monthly injections of 125 mg hydroxyprogesterone caproate, or 10 mg/day sl-oral dydrogesterone.

Month 4: If breasts are not yet developing (budding), given continued health, increase estrogen dosage to the following: twice-monthly injections of 40 mg estradiol valerate, or 4 mg estradiol cypionate. Also, take 1-3 mg/day sl-oral estradiol or 2-4 mg/day sl-oral estradiol valerate or a single 0.075-0.1 mg transdermal estradiol film changed weekly. If these injectibles are not available, employ 2 0.1mg transdermal estradiol films changed twice weekly, offset (e.g., change the first film Monday morning and Thursday evening; change the second film Wednesday morning and Saturday evening), or 6mg/day sl-oral estradiol, or 9 mg/day sl-oral estradiol valerate. Note that injectables or films are much preferable to administration of the entire estrogen therapy orally. Do not increase estrogen at this time if there is currently progress in breast development.

Month 5: If androgens are still a problem (continued scalp hair recession, frequent spontaneous erections, etc.), given continued health, increase anti-androgens to the following: 200 mg/day spironolactone plus larger fractional tablet (0.1-1mg)/day finasteride. If spironolactone is not available but cyproterone acetate is, employ 25 mg/day cyproterone acetate.

Month 6: If breasts are not yet developing, given continued health, increase progesterone/progestin dosage to the following: 300-400 mg/day oral progesterone, or twice-monthly injections of 125mg hydroxyprogesterone caproate, or 20 mg/day sl-oral dydrogesterone.

Month 7: If breasts are not yet developing, given continued health, increase estrogen dosage to the following: twice-monthly injections of 60mg estradiol valerate, or 6mg of estradiol cypionate. Also, take 2-4 mg/day sl-oral estradiol or 3-6mg/day sl-oral estradiol valerate or a single 0.1 mg transdermal estradiol film changed every 4-7 days. If these injectables are not available, employ 3-4 0.1 mg transdermal estradiol films each changed twice weekly, offset, or 8mg/day sl-oral estradiol, or 12 mg/day sl-oral estradiol valerate (do not attempt to run up the oral doses in the same ramp as other deliveries; if this dose of orals is not doing the job, it is quite unlikely that adding more will help). Do not increase estrogen at this time if there is currently progress in breast development.

Tess,

As we dissect the brain further everyday, and locate the
amygdala, thalami, and basal ganglia, I think of the blow to your
temporal lobe. I think of Kluver-Bucy, a pair of men who identified
an eponymous syndrome that affected the area of the brain
where you were assaulted. These patients became hypersexual,
hyperoral, and very submissive. I think of a father figure who
used these symptoms to his advantage and then killed you.
Fathers do these sorts of things, you know. That initial blow to
your brain was not the death of you. As we dissect further, the
basal ganglia tells the rest of the story. It's speckled with darkness
due to a lack of oxygen. It is a tell-tale sign that you were in need
of oxygen. Strangulation, suffocation, carbon monoxide poisoning.
The story is beginning to unravel itself. And it's a story of your
family, Tess.

Understanding,
Adrien

Without Anesthesia

My Tess,

Night by night, those killers are growing more suspicious of me. I wear my necklace of your heart beneath my undershirt for fear that it will arouse more controversy, more animosity if seen. The tissue rubs against my chest and sends shivers through my body. Electricity. It's as alive for me as I know you are, somewhere else. I think one of those killers saw me touch the silver chain as I do so, unconsciously, now and again. He quickly turned away though. He dare not catch my gaze. I've grown fucking hard. Tough and merciless. A mercenary for you. I no longer participate in your killing. I don't. I don't cut. I merely observe what they do. We participated in a blood ceremony before we first cut you and none of us can be disbanded from another. We share this secret that is you. They cannot let me go, nor can I they. It's a brotherhood. It's a ceremony of sacrifice. I'm thinking about the strangulation, the suffocation. Your brain cannot lie. It's hard evidence. The others cut, merely to cut, to see and identify what they have not seen before. But, Tess, I'm trying to understand you, to read you, to comprehend a history that is so much darker than you yourself could have narrated: Your father is always furtively waiting for you. You acquiesce each time. Your mother knows this. But she's not tough, she gives in to what she sees every night. But that night, that night of infamy, you had had it. You could no longer go through with it. He understood this, saw your inflexibility, your hardness. And, if he couldn't have you to enjoy, no one else could. Suffocation was then tantamount to dispossession of your body for the Other's enjoyment. No one else should enjoy you if he couldn't. During the course of suffocation, your head is bludgeoned against the bedside table. Your brain cannot lie. Tess, this is your story, your ill-fated destiny.

Always sorry,
Your Reader

ZAMORANO WAS GROWING SICKER by the day. He was moved to the Intensive Care Unit as a precautionary measure that, as the doctors had now realized, was inevitable. His illness confounded the medical staff, a sepsis whose source could not be identified. His fevers waxed and waned, as did his oxygen saturation and white blood cell counts. He was an enigma for the physicians and a curiosity for the medical students. The students would eye his menagerie as does a baby lion its protected prey. They wanted him to themselves to solve as a puzzle and then spit him out when he had been chewed and savored.

Tess eyed Zamorano differently and her instinctual gaze pierced her fellow students' every time she saw them looking at his room. This time, she was the lioness that would do all to protect her wounded child. She had successfully managed to secure a spot in an internal medicine rotation in the wards to keep an eye on her Savior. She wanted to show Zamorano that she, and only she, knew how he felt. The statement that he had remarked before he was transferred to the ICU reverberated in her head: You cannot possibly know, you cannot possibly know...and Tess's obsession would not allow it to be dispensed so easily.

Although Tess was confined to the Ward, comprised of the hospital rooms in which the old man had recently resided, the accessibility of the ICU to these rooms and her liminal status as a medical student did not prevent her from entering it. She relished the opportunity of visiting Zamorano after her daily rounds with the Attending. She lived for this. She realized that he now embodied for her the patient whose body she must learn as her own.

But it was at dusk when Zamorano seemed to come alive and hold brief conversations with her. She would don a white mask, as visitors to his room would be required, and enter quietly, obeisantly, like a thief entering a room that she had studied in some detail. She didn't mean to surprise, but she was always caught off-guard by Zamorano and made to feel like the violated. The trespasser as the trespassed. That is what she felt like every time.

One particular night, the old man felt more vibrant than ever. His fever had subsided and his white blood cell count was beginning to decrease. None of the medical staff knew what to think of this miraculous turn-around but, as they themselves had acknowledged, there were certain scientific mysteries that would always elude them. It was their duty merely to safeguard against the majority of the illnesses and let fate play with the others. They were simply pleased that there was a change of fortune for this old man. The hospital could not sustain another dying patient, without insurance, in a room whose rent exceeded that of the richest lofts in Manhattan. They were pleased that this patient would not die here and skew the morbidity and mortality statistics that was bound to determine the overall rank of the hospital. They were very pleased.

As usual, Tess entered Zamorano's room furtively, having donned one of the white, aseptic masks that were laid on a cart outside the room. She didn't look as ridiculous in this mask as she did in those orange duck-masks she was required to wear for the TB patients. She realized that she cared about her appearance in front of this old man and content that her hair had assumed a more pleasing shape than when it was first cut. She had worked on her makeup skills as well and, although far from perfect, it was acceptable, passing for what she had hoped to accomplish.

Zamorano's eyes, though closed, darted towards her like a heliotropic plant to a gesture of movement. Tess nearly jumped in place and took a step backwards. She almost fell, but managed to catch herself.

"Dear Lady Tess," the old man's now vivacious timbre seemed to echo in that hermetic space, "I feel so alive today as if I've been reborn. This darkness no longer surrounds me. Strengthened by your light, I can continue. My sickness, no one can truly understand from where it comes and how it feels."

How many stabs could Tess endure? Tears swelled in her eyes again as the memories of that ill-fated statement returned. All that she could remark to the old man was that he was too kind and that she would return later to see him. She really couldn't continue to speak more at that moment and knew that it would be a while before she returned again to see Zamorano. There really was no other way out. The plunge was inevitable. Tess shivered at the thought but was ready.

My poor Tess,

When will this horror stop? As if dissecting your brain was not bad enough, one of the bastard killers mentioned that your eye remained to be studied and structures within it identified. What more can I possibly say? We will have used you, the last of you, every scrap, down to the bone, until you have become waste, mashed tissue, worse than vomit, in this charnel house. You poor thing. One day, I will kill those killers for you. I am your mercenary, though you need not pay me. That myocardium around my neck is more precious than anything this world can offer to me. They say that the eye is a vista into the soul. Those killers will be taking that away from me shortly. You can no longer gaze at me and I at you. Your pupils are so eroded and ashenly hazy, but I can still see you, see your soul, as clear as the bluest waters. Oedipus gouged his own eyes so as not to see his own projected sins. But the enucleation made him look inward and see his crime more intently. So it is with you, Tess. They will have enucleated you, it is true, but it is their crime that will become manifest. They want to get rid of the evidence, get rid of the witnessed eyes that saw. But don't you see? You have tricked them. You have managed to dupe them at their own game. A bait and switch. The eyes for the teeth. The real evidence remains, Tess. Your teeth.

Smiling (like the Cheshire Cat),
A.

Adrien threw the last of her remains there, in the cold, damp earth with which he was so familiar now. He had decorated this space with portraits that he had drawn of her and dug it deeper. Lithographs, watercolors, and even a wax effigy of her so that she could be buried as herself, as whole. The teeth seemed so insignificant in the scheme of things, but it remained as evidence, that she was cut up and mutilated by those killers. He wished that he could be buried with her here so that part of his aliveness could be transmitted to her by osmosis. The two would survive together in this repose, this small castle in the earth, which would protect them from the evils of this world.

Adrien would not touch her dead tissues again after he had covered the grave. He had seen the last of her, had taken whatever memories he had of her. There was nothing else to possess, nothing else to destroy. He was sure of his actions now. He would resurrect her. Give her a new identity.

Dusk was calling him home. He wished he could remain there, above her remains, and keep vigil for as long as possible. He covered the opening of the grave in fertile soil. The small shovel that he had used over the past few months had given him such callous hands and scars. But he relished the proof of toil that he had undergone. He wanted more.

"I lend myself to the social game, I pose, I want you to know that I am posing..."

–Roland Barthes
Camera Lucida

"When there is nothing left to burn, you have to set your self on fire."

–Torquil Campbell
Your Ex-Lover is Dead

The Second Cut

Fragments of Damaged Life:
The Collected Papers of Anton Gadomsky*
(Excerpt)

My name is Anton Gadomsky. I was born on July 4th, 1922, in Hollywood, California. Fireworks did not announce my arrival. Fireworks did not set me free. My olfactory senses hinted at a different notion of freedom. These senses were already keen from birth. The illegal substances simply refined them. I should thank the Prohibition for that. Bootleggers and commoners alike were flagrantly violating the Volstead Act. My mother was no different, disrespecting everything in sight. I don't know about my father. I never met that fucking bastard.

My mother was a heavy drinker who would procure her liquor either from bootleggers or from illegal speakeasies, hidden in basements. She was the worst of them. A temperamental drunk who ruined everything in sight. I wouldn't be surprised if she were drinking and smoking when the midwife delivered me that night. I'm sure she had made a wish at that moment. To make me the most miserable individual in the world. Her wish would come true.

My mother was an actress. Well, sort of. She aspired to be a white version of Minto Cato, the Black Vaudevillian theatrical performer at the time. I don't know what my mother saw in her. But she had her picture up, with Cato's big, brown eyes staring at me from the refrigerator door whenever I came to get milk. I was eight. Cato's eyes gestured that mother was up to no good, that she was as crazy and deluded as I knew she was. Mother, however, would smoke her Lucky Strikes being won over by the

---

* Edited and Foreword by Daniel Rubenstein, M.D. Fragments of Damaged Life: The Collected Papers of Anton Gadomsky. Prometheus Press (Los Angeles: 1999)

slogan that she could become slim again: "Reach for a Lucky instead of a sweet." Her pregnancy had disturbed her pristine figure. I was the cause of her not getting auditions for plays and silent films. She wished that she could smoke me straight to hell.

I was fucking tenacious though. I clung to this earth and learned as much as I could from it. I thought that being born on the 4th was fate, that it should confer some freedom on me. With this in mind, I flouted rules and took notes from my mother, the biggest law-breaker that Hollywood had seen. She would buy her liquor illegally, as everyone did in those years, and acted as if this liquor were stolen from her, which, I guess, was true. I learned these unspoken truths from her: that what was invisible was in some ways more truthful and real than what was actually shown, that one was in the right when others told him otherwise. She was a progressive anti-prohibitionist, a precursor of the ultra-liberal 60s activist. She was freedom and I was merely a by-product of what she represented. My 4th of July theory quickly went to hell. It was she who would fly.

In our small apartment on Ivar St., my mother practiced lines for parts that she had no chance of landing. She was no Greta Garbo or Clara Bow, nor did she aspire to be. But she practiced lines befitting them with the ridiculous gestures and pantomimes of Vaudevillian acts like Cato's. It was obscene and perverted, the way she chopped those scenes and made them as ridiculous and stupid as they ought to have been. In a way, she was one of the best actresses there was. Uninhibited, playful, and never self-conscious. In those days, though, she merely turned people off. They were not ready for the independence that she claimed, for the butchy nature that she represented. It was the 1920s, for God's sake. Women were not supposed to have dicks.

She even used to parade around the apartment in

black face, imitating Minto Cato, whom she absolutely adored. Our threadbare apartment was the setting of a regular minstrel show, and my mother its one-woman performer. She looked ridiculous, her white body contrasting horribly with her black face. But when I questioned her, she would say that this was precisely the point. That a good actress, through her performance, would make you believe anything. That the more fake she looked on the outside, the more profound her triumph would be if she made the spectator forget her appearance through her good acting. However, I saw and forgot nothing. My mother looked as ridiculous as ever. But she had the strength to continue with her exaggerated gestures and pantomimes without giving a damn about what people thought. I liked that about her.

I remember that our place was a shit-hole. My mother had all sorts of garbage around the house, old magazines detailing the accounts of the actresses whom she admired, empty cigarette boxes, and bottles of old whiskey, among other things. She had even tried to make her own liquor in the apartment, but a small fire made her realize that she was no chemist. So she continued to visit the speak-easies and get her fill that way. I knew that she was not far from hell.

She wasn't a bad mother, I suppose. I had freedom. So I learned quickly and would imitate what she did and react as she would. She was always behind on the rent, but the way that she would get away with this was utter genius. She would make our landlady, Ms. Imogene Walker, laugh hysterically when she came to collect the overdue rent. Ms. Walker was a mulatto who had inherited her property from her white father. When she would come over, my mother would dress up like Minto Cato and dance the most hysterical dance that I ever seen [sic]. She wasn't trying to be funny, but it all looked so ridiculously stupid. So exaggerated that it made the whole world look artificial, making you realize that nothing was real. I think that's what Ms. Walker liked. To forget that she was always being discriminated against despite her inherited wealth. She wanted to forget her problems and mother was a perfect vehicle for that. Ms. Walker did not want to lose this little goldmine of hers, this thing in the world that made her laugh so hard that she could forget about what really bothered her about this world. No, a few months' late rent was worth this state of oblivion. It was better than any drug or liquor that the bootleggers were dealing to people. Ms. Walker had her very own dealer in her apartment building.

In order to pay for our necessities, mother worked as a seamstress. It suited her lifestyle, as she was able to work at home and keep an eye out for me. Not that she cared about me or anything. But, at least, it made her conscience feel more at ease, which helped her acting. She would get her business mainly from a local theatre company, where clothes were continually in need of mending. She would also try to create her own designs and sell these, but she rarely got lucky. Hers were always at once too sophisticated and gaudy, like something that had been mistakenly sewn on another respectable dress so that it looked vulgar and erie [sic]. She didn't know when to stop. She wasn't a bad designer at all, but she would compulsively sew and sew until a monster was born. It looked grotesque.

I continued to live like this, until mother became horribly sick when I was eleven. She was drinking as heavily as ever. The quality of the liquor was getting worse and the concentration of the alcohol was increasing, mainly because there was no regulation of alcohol during those days. I could see that she was turning more yellow by the day. When she would dress up like Cato, which she continued to do, she looked worse than a black version of Frankenstein. She had sallow

eyes, a black face, and a white body. I couldn't look at
her anymore. It made me sick. But when I would tell her
that she should go see a doctor, she would laugh at me in
a serious tone and say, "What does a kid know anyway?"
Although I didn't care whether my mother lived or died, I
had grown accustomed to her, and my life, although not
comfortable, was at least predictable. I liked that.

Mother was getting sicker by the day and Ms. Walker,
who was always in a jovial mood whenever she saw her,
became worried. "And, honey, what is it with those yellow
eyes of yours? I can't have you parading in this apartment
as Minto Cato, looking like that. Now can I?" She would
try to laugh this off, but you could tell that she knew
that she was losing her precious gem. Ms. Walker, bless
her soul, was such a kind woman that she even hired
a personal doctor to look after my mother, two days a
week. His name was Dr. Arthur Goldman, a Jewish man in
his late 50s, who was as compassionate as our landlady.
He wore a pince-nez. He was balding. And his eyes were
always so kind and gentle. The perfect picture of a doctor.
He had taken a liking to me as I to him.

Although Dr. Goldman was married, his wife was
unable to conceive. He looked on me as a son and
would allow me to do medical procedures that would be
unimaginable for a boy my age. I would play a role in
the daily injections of my mother. "Not too forceful now,
Anton. You don't want the needle to break." He was the
only one to call me Anton, the only person to consider me
as a person of my own. Through him, I learned what little
I knew about my mother's body. I had felt no affection
from her, but Dr. Goldman allowed me to feel what that
affection could feel like. Through his firm and guided
palpation, I was able to feel mother's enlarged liver and
spleen swimming in a large sea of fluid. He would extend
mother's wrists and, once this was done, her wrists would
continue to flex, like a bird flapping its wings. He said

69.

that this was "asterixis," a sign that mother's brain cells were being damaged. An indication that the liver couldn't break down the ammonia that was so harmful to it. He allowed me to hear her rapid heart rate and her coarse, shallow breathing. Mother had never appeared so sick and so personal to me as this. I preferred it to our previous encounters. She seemed so much more alive despite her impending death. I envied the attention that Dr. Goldman and Ms. Walker were giving to her just because she was so sick. That's when I first realized that I could use this tactic to generate sympathy for being sick. I was even reaping some of these benefits through her sick body.

Dr. Goldman knew that Mother's illness would not turn out well, either. You could tell that he was nervous by the way he pushed up his pince-nez whenever the topic of Mother's prognosis would come up. He told us that she had cirrhosis of the liver, that Mother's normal liver cells had become damaged and replaced by scar tissue. He tried to pin no moral judgments on her but instead blamed the Prohibition on what it had done to her. My mother's sallow eyes, which were becoming more yellow every day, had now completely lost their luster and simply looked at Dr. Goldman like a puppy's sick eyes right before death. Mother had completely lost her energy. She was continually itching herself and her stomach was beginning to get larger. Dr. Goldman told Ms. Walker and me that these were signs that the liver was slowly dying, that it could not do its job properly. I simply looked at him without a hint as to what I was feeling, which was nothing at all. But Ms. Walker was sobbing as if Mother had already died. She would squeeze me harder each day as if her strength was an indication that Mother's death would soon arrive. "Oh, baby, baby," she would say to me, "what will we ever do without your mother? Without her precious gift of making us laugh?" I looked at her as I normally would, without saying much, and pretended that I didn't understand what she was referring to. I had that way about me, making myself appear stupid and ignorant to others, while I was calculating things that no one could imagine. Since no attention was ever placed on me, I could get away with anything without causing suspicion. I was always in the background, while Mother was performing her center-stage antics. That is, until she got seriously sick with the cirrhosis.

In her illness, however, Mother became more of a spectacle than ever. She would lie in her bed, wearing an imitation Boue Soeurs nightgown, trimmed with filet lace, which she herself had designed. She would hold a celluloid and black organza folding hand fan, a Coco Chanel look-alike. Her eyes were now blazing yellow. And her hair was matted and utterly disheveled. Although it had been a while since she had bathed herself, she smelled sweet and did not have that sickly smell that we associate with old and dying people. There was a lot to take in when you saw her. But amidst this sensory overload, there was a sort of calmness, like a skiff in calm waters, which made it pleasant to be beside her. Don't get me wrong. I still did not like Mother. But, like I said before, I loved the familiarity of an unchanging universe that accommodated my laziness.

On the eve of July 4, 1934, the day I turned 12, Mother finally flew. Fireworks motioned her to go, to follow them away from this earth. I was looking out of the window at that moment. I knew she would be going and wanted to see her this free, shattered and sprayed all over Hollywood, like the star that she had hoped to become. I focused on the Catherine Wheel, with its pretty colors in a spreading whirl of fire. I almost saw Mother in its flames, the way she was swirling and dancing. So free. But in a moment, this image had turned to a hell of fire, with Mother as a stand-in for Saint Catherine of Alexandria as she was being tortured on this breaking wheel. I felt sad for Mother. But she was free, in one way or another, while I was still bound to this fucking hell.

When Mother died, I inherited her personal physician as my surrogate father. Dr. Arthur Goldman and his wife became my new parents and I their boy, the child they never could have had. I was sad, not because I had lost Mother, but because my life would follow a new routine. Although the Goldman's doted on me and treated me as a newly-found treasure trove, I did not relish my new position. I wanted that sick kind of love. The love that you give to someone when you know that they're going from this earth, when you realize that they may be no more, of the shame of thinking for a moment that you wanted them dead. Dr. Goldman, now father to me, tried to kindle my interest in medicine since he had seen my natural inkling towards it. He tried to train me in both the art and science of medicine—not only how to inject, but also what to say when injecting. Not only how to listen to the heart, but also how to respond to the patient who is having his most intimate organ heard. He taught me all of these things. I absorbed it like a dry sponge to wet blood.

I learned a great deal from my new and only father that I knew. He grew fonder of me each day, although he recognized that I showed little emotion to anyone. He thought that my childhood had led me to this point, to the empty nature of love. He did all he could to understand me, but I shut him out, as I did everyone. He had patience.

On my 16th birthday, father came to me with an oblong box. It had a strange shape to it and was old. "Son, this is your birthday present," he said. I opened the box and held the small dagger that it contained. "For A," it said. It looked so old, this dagger, as if transported from another place, where nymphs and centaurs ruled. I held it and felt its corrugated edges, its rough texture. "It was my great great grandfather's, who inherited it from another place, from someone whom we will never know. It dates back to the 16th Century. I'd like to give it to you for posterity's sake." I sighed, as I took this all in. It was too much for me, this history that was now mine to protect. "But what about the A," I said afectionately [*sic*]. "Did you inscribe it for me?" "No, my dear," he responded. "The men in this family of Goldman's have all carried first names beginning with the letter 'A'. "It was providence that brought you to us, my dear Anton. The 'A' which will protect you. It will be the 'A' with which you'll die."

"In this condensation of musk and merde, we once again encounter the connection between perfume and the smell of shit."

–Dominique Laporte
History of Shit

"The seducer knows how to let the signs hang."

–Jean Baudrillard
Seduction

The Third Cut

Ms. Tessla Ferrara,

It has truly been a pleasure to have written about you in the first
paper assigned to us in our Cinema Studies 201 Course -- Modern
Italian Cinema: Federico Fellini to Luchino Visconti. I spent
the entire night writing the twenty-five page paper, amidst the
votives, drinking bitter Campari, and keeping vigil over your
textual corpus. And how magnificent it is! You are truly the
brightest starlet in Italian avant-garde cinema today. And you
do not realize the power with which you captivate your viewers.
I remain in awe, Ms. Ferrara. After attending a screening of
your film, Rapina, the skewed postmodern feminist variation of
Bonnie and Clyde, I understood that you are a star that has not
realized her potential. As you know, the film involves a feigned
hold-up at a liquor store, a prank, invented by two college girls
who dress up as Jackie O look-alikes, merely to make fun of the
institution of crime. No real guns, no real intentions, just play.
But a customer in the liquor store, who himself carries a gun, sees
"real" guns in the hands of these girls (one of them, Francesca,
played brilliantly by you) and begins to shoot. Tragedies soon
unfold. He sees intentions, when there is none, and "reads" crime
in this visual hallucination, when this is a closed text. Signs of
the real, as Jean Baudrillard himself would say, substitute for
the real itself, without clearly demarcating the original. But you,
Ms. Ferrara, are the ultimate simulacra in the film. As a copy of
Jackie O (recalling her Warholian technical reproducibility), you
supplant this original and erase the difference, making us ask
whether Jackie O, herself, is not a copy of you. Your gestures are
impeccable down to the way you demurely state your intentions
to the clerk: "Your money or your life, Sir," without a hint of
bravado. In this scene, you are re-enacting "a" Jackie O (among

many copies) through your character Francesca who is being played by your "self," Tessla Ferrara. Twice removed and doubly brilliant. I hope that you realize how profound your undertaking is and the dimension of postmodernity that you bring to this film.

Sincerely,
Adriana Eyre

Note: I am eagerly awaiting the screening of more of your films to be held at the University this week.

Ms. Tessla Ferrara,

I cannot disengage myself of the image of Francesca, the
character you enacted in Rapina. I identify with her completely.
She appears to be quite restrained in her emotions, but is able to
create a persona that is more real than real itself. "Your money
or your life." She does not intend to kill the clerk, and her tone is
playful, undecided. It's as if it were neither about money or life,
but about a third element to which she is only privy. But then
she is shot, at the moment when she is about to confess to the
joke. At the moment when she wants to say that it is not about
either either/or, it ends with the or: her life. Everything has
led up to this. We viewers see Francesca metamorphose slowly
but deliberately. As a shy girl interested in the film media and
completely enamored of Jackie O's celebrity status to one who,
although still demure, is willing to take risks, Francesca projects
herself in this role superbly. (In my paper, I contrasted your role
to that of Maddalena in Visconti's Bellissima.) A case of (mis)
identification with the Other; a telephone call that was aborted as
soon as it was connected to the Other (Sorry, wrong number).[*] In
the conclusion of the film, although gunned down so horrifically,
one can sense that Francesca's toil and dreams have not been for
nothing. A double negative that emerges triumphantly and makes
her something more than she is. No, I cannot disengage myself of
Francesca and, by extension, you, Ms. Ferrara.

––––––––––––––

[*] Speaking of wrong numbers, you may enjoy Anatole Litvak's
Sorry, Wrong Number (1946). The film details the life of a woman
with cardiac neurosis who is confined to her bed, communicating
with others only through her bedside telephone.

Forever in awe of your images,
Adriana

Note: I will be viewing Prosopagnosia tomorrow night and am
utterly excited.

AS SHE FILLED THE SYRINGE AGAIN, this time with her feces, Tess knew that she had advanced to the next level, that there would be no turning back. Her knowledge of medical illness had grown and, by extension and necessity, so had her means of applying this. Accessibility to the medical supplies had not been a problem. No one was really attentive to the medical students. They were extras, as in a film, there to advance the idea that the medical institution was viable, that there were actual students to be taught, that reality pervaded and propelled this infrastructure. The medical staff was like actors who had to make this believable for the patients, the audience, or the entire spectacle would fall apart. The spectators were dazzled by this phantasmagoria and could not care less to comprehend it. Tess realized that medical students filled in this void of the extra, a hinge without which the entire venture would be found out for the fraud that it was.

Tess did not feel like an extra today. It was as if she had walked on stage and noticed that the props were real. The needle had nearly pierced her skin when she came to uncap it, and the syringe had nearly fallen apart when she came to pull it. This was reality. The feces were another problem altogether. Tess had collected a sample of her stool, diluted it with water, and then placed it in the syringe. She had cringed at the idea of intravenously injecting herself with feces, comprised of *E. coli* and Enterococcus faecalis, among other potentially lethal bacteria, but knew no other way of simulating septic shock. Her thoughts now turned to Zamorano and the disgust she had felt at seeing his colostomy bag full of feces. That was so long ago and she had learned so much since. She must do this for him. Zamorano had undergone such a disease process and she must follow his course. He must know that she herself could feel, could empathize with him, even if this could be the death of her. The old man had somehow recovered from his illness, without an etiology to explain his symptoms. Tess was sure that once the bacteria had been identified in her, heavy doses of effective antibiotics, like Vancomycin and Rocephin, would resolve her symptoms and free her from the disease. After all, most patients did recover from their illnesses, whether due to conventional medicine or the acknowledged, albeit bastardized, simulator, the placebo. In her short time at the hospital, Tess had seen miracles borne out of the placebo effect. Nothing short of the faith that the audience had placed in this cinematic apparatus, this was the real placebo.

Whether it was estradiol, hydroxyprogesterone, or, for her last venture, air, the needle was always bevel up. She tired to be as mechanical as possible, giving due diligence to her sterile techniques. She realized that today, shit, literally, had infested the entire aseptic routine that she had assiduously regimented since entering medical school. She was blaspheming the organization of hygiene, all that the Occupational Safety and Health Administration had worked so hard to foster for future medical students and physicians. This was the ultimate Hippocratic oath and she had taken it beyond what was necessary.

She hoped that her feces would not clump the syringe. The idea of having to dilute it again sickened her, and she wished that there could be another way to accomplish what she intended. She knew that this was by far the easiest and least conspicuous of ways. It would be very difficult for her to be detected. At this moment, the thought of bacteria proliferating and multiplying in her took hold of her imagination and she laid the fecal-filled syringe next to her bedside table. She began to take deep breaths as if preparing herself for the onslaught of a panic attack that would momentarily seize her. Fortunately, her obsessed mind got a hold of Zamorano once again. His plaintive tone, his yearning to become better again, for someone to empathize with him. Tess needed to feel as he felt. Heroically and without further thought, she plunged the needle into her left median cubital vein. Shit had now gained entry into the most coveted of transport systems and it flowed. It had invaded the pristine stream. Tess did not look back.

Fragments of Damaged Life:
The Collected Papers of Anton Gadomsky[*]
(Excerpt)

I wish that I could go to hell. I want to tell this to my dead mother as I drink another whiskey to commemorate the 40th anniversary of her death. I sit in a nearly empty tavern on Hollywood Boulevard. I drink round after round of scotch blended whiskey. I prefer J & B to no other. I rarely talk to anyone these days. As I recollect memories of the old days, I realize that Mother was a moonshiner. I had seen her make liquor in our house, before she had nearly set it to flames. She had probably taken this work with her to small-scale stills when I was sleeping at night. She worked under the light of moon. The Devil gave her hit after hit.

I realize that my dream has come true. I am in fucking hell, holed up to rot in all eternity here. No one loves me. I don't love anyone. I wish that I could kill myself. I can't. I need to be sick. I need to play this role that has been thrust upon me. To die would defeat this purpose. I think to myself, how did life turn out like this? So fucked-up, for me. Why was I cast for this part? Why do I need spectators? Is it Mother? Was it her illness that has made me who I am? Am I doing this all for her?

I think about my last hospital visit, about a week ago. I still feel the penetrating gaze of the ER physician, the way he thought that I had tried to sexually gratify myself with the bottle of whiskey that was broken inside my rectum. I want to tell him, Doctor, this was all planned. I had meant to break that whiskey bottle inside of me so that you could retrieve part of it from my rectum. Now you aren't so smart, are you? I led him down a pretty

* Edited and Foreword by Daniel Rubenstein, M.D.
Fragments of Damaged Life: The Collected Papers of Anton Gadomsky Prometheus Press (Los Angeles: 1999)

good story, in West Hollywood, in the gay neighborhood, so that he would think I was one of them, that all I wanted was sexual gratification from a whiskey bottle. How fucking narrow minded you are, Doctor. I was simply playing a role and you bought my acting. Mother would be so proud.

He fished for the bottleneck, this doctor, Smith or Wilson, I don't know anymore. He had some generic name. Not like mine. Anton. Smith or Wilson, he retrieved that shard of glass with a tissue wrapped around the neck, and told me that wasn't I so lucky. Next time it would not fare so well for me. He realized the slip that he made and changed the topic. Too quickly. Of course I know what you're thinking, Doctor, I had wanted to tell him. Don't be so quick to judge. I don't need to fuck myself with a whiskey bottle to get off. I can get love the natural way, with people, you know. Or am I deluding myself? Can someone love me for myself and not for what I have done to myself? Maybe I'm afraid to find out. It is better to fake it than to truly put my feelings out there. I don't want to be rejected again.

After I was discharged from the ER, I knew that I wouldn't return here for an encore performance. I'm afraid my show is a one-night stunt [*sic*]. I wanted to holler at the spectators and medical staff in the ER. You either make it to the show or you don't. There are no encores and no refunds for your sympathy. That's mine to keep, dear viewers. So I ambled out of the ER with the penetrating gaze of the doctors behind me. The balmy, Southern California weather welcomed me into its arms and prompted me to think of my next destination, my next one-man show. I knew that my act was done here.

Tessla (can I call you that?),

I'm astounded, to say the least. Prosopagnosia screened last
night to a packed theater of hipsters. The subject matter was a bit
elusive to me at first, the origins of the neurological process very
discomfiting. I had never heard of such a thing. Prosopagnosia,
namely misrecognition of faces as a result of head trauma (as
far as I understood from the film), is an utterly fascinating but
disturbing concept to me. But, Tessla, your cinematic brilliance
brought this to life as if I were one who suffered from this disease.
Let me provide a synopsis of the film as this helps me articulate
my thoughts about your performance. The visual corpus
surrounds a couple (Alessandra, played phenomenally by you)
who is lasciviously enamored of each other, with so many scenes of
cunnilingus, fellatio, and penetration that I felt I had mistakenly
walked into an earlier pornographic film in which you may have
starred (the scenes were quite artistic and never vulgar). But
I retrospectively understood that these scenes were meant to
illustrate that you were true lovers, meant for one another since
birth. And then, one stormy night, you two have too much alcohol
to drink after a protracted amount of lovemaking and your car
veers off a cliff, not exactly killing you, but causing you both to
sustain similar, severe head trauma. A bit unbelievable, I know,
but your acting, Tessla, allows this cinematic diegesis to unfold
seamlessly and realistically. You two are transported to different
hospitals, without IDs, and found to have amnesia, having lost
long-term memory. More importantly, it is later determined that
you have had trauma to a portion of your brain responsible for
recognizing faces (the scientific jargon that the doctor spews to
explain this process remains unclear to me but I plan to research
it). It appears that you can see and recognize certain parts of

the face, but not the entirety. (I am still uncertain as to whether this brain abnormality actually exists). But, regardless, you two are now separated and will remain so for about a third of the film. You are now leading separate lives. You, a clerk at a small Italian boutique in Sienna. He, a bartender at a nightclub in the same city. Jobs that don't really necessitate recognition of specific faces, enabling interaction with anonymous customers. But life is tough for both of you. I can read the longing in your face, your melancholy disposition, though you are not cognizant of a past life with your wonderful lover. (I felt your pain and cried a few times during the screening.—I know that adept film critics should be able to separate fiction from reality, but I simply can't with you.) You both realize that something is "missing," besides the nebulous faces that you encounter daily. But you, Tessla, you take that further. I feel yearning in your eyes, a yearning for a jouissance that knows no boundaries. One day you enter the bar in which your lover works, and, though you cannot recognize what appears to you as a reproducible face, you hear the voice and smell the smell. At that point, the memory of your lover, as relayed to you by his scent, infinitely reproduces more signs, the smell of his Cartier cologne mixed with damp sweat, the musky smell of the shampoo that he uses after vigorous sex, and so forth, until you "see" his face in the scenes of your multitudinous lovemaking episodes. (These synesthetic scenes were done brilliantly with cuts and montages that made me visually "see" the smell.) His voice is now reverberating and you seem to hear him groan as he normally did while thrusting inside of you, and you know that he is your lover. The same process occurs for him as well. Oh, Tessla. You had me in tears and I had never cried for anyone as much as I did for your character, Alessandra. It was like the ending of Chaplin's City Lights, when the formerly blind woman whom the tramp loves (the woman having had an operation to correct her sight), hears his voice and is able to now "match" it to his body. However, as the film concludes with this denouement, we are unsure as to how this woman will respond. Will she love him as much as he loves her, knowing now that he is a tramp? Having seen his demeanor and rank in society, will she reject him? I had cried for those two characters, their precarious destinies. But for you, Tessla/Alessandra, I cried for a different reason. For a joy that you would soon experience again and one that would be greater for your having had reclaimed it after so many years. As I walked out of the University cinema, I felt that others were looking at my swollen, red eyes for having cried so much for you. They didn't really say anything but, nonetheless, they looked and figured it out. At that moment, I felt that I had been your martyr, a Christ-like figure that had died in your diegesis so that you could live and perform again. I would die again, if I had to.

Indebted,
Adriana

THIS TIME SHE WALKED into the Emergency Department room as a patient. She was no longer identified as Tess. The wipe board had reduced her to a woman in Room 4 with fever, chest pain, and tachycardia, and she was given a wristband with an associated barcode. Her medications would be scanned as well and linked to this code. She had liked the anonymity of the experience. No one had recognized her as Tess, although she had rotated here a few months ago. It was only a matter of time, as she was bound to run into one of the nurses with whom she had worked. Abigail, her previous resident, was off today. Tess had made sure to verify her absence. She did not want her admission to the hospital to become a spectacle, more than it would already be. The obvious choice would have been to choose a different ER, but she had to ensure that Zamorano would be aware of her admission to the wards. Tess did not want to lose sight of her goals and having Zamorano nearby would be a reminder of that.

It had taken a day for the fever to manifest itself. The day that she had injected herself, Tess had tried to busy herself with her duties in the wards. She did not want to dwell on her riskiest venture so far. However, as the afternoon approached, she felt fatigued and noticed dull chest pains. Her plan was to present herself to the ER as soon as she felt that she had experienced all that she could before the onslaught of the sepsis, but before the entire process turned lethal. There was a fine line separating the two, and Tess felt that she was still inexperienced. She certainly had been conservative in her past deliberations of how to proceed, but knew that the nature of the sepsis would not tolerate such apprehension.

She waited in Room 4. It was cold and damp. Lying in the gurney made the experience more palatable. Here she was. Waiting as a patient does for a doctor to cure her ailments. She relished the experience that she was feeling as they had done, these thousands of patients who had come before her in this very room, perhaps having lain in this identical gurney, but with the difference that she had subjected herself to this. Zamorano's image flashed in her head. He was probably recovering well now, while she was about to undergo a shock that she had never experienced. She imagined him coming into her hospital room once she was admitted. He would tell her that she does now know what his sepsis felt like, having experienced the sepsis herself. This would the ultimate compliment from him, the ultimate gesture that they were in some way connected now. She had done this for him, her gift to him.

Her vitals were taken. Her body temperature was 102.8 F, pulse 118, respirations 22, and blood pressure 75/55. When the ER nurse had told her this, she had cringed, as she knew that she was experiencing the first wave of the sepsis. Her blood pressure was dangerously low. She recalled the pathophysiology of sepsis as was taught to her in medical school and knew the steps that would soon follow. Who knew that, at that time, she was rehearsing a dialogue, a process that she would actually experience. A pan culture was ordered, as was a litany of tests to detect the etiology of the infection. She was also complaining of chest pain now, a feature that she had not counted on and one that could potentially devastate her plans. She jolted at these revelations as she prepared herself for the role that she had thrust upon herself. She could not turn back.

Tessla/Alessandra,

You'd be happy to know that I did my research, delving into
Adams and Victor's Principles of Neurology (apparently regarded
as the comprehensive neurological text, the librarian told me) to
determine if prosopagnosia is an actual brain abnormality. The
librarian looked at me perplexingly, realizing that I was most
likely from the art department. I think that my flowing, floral
dress, with the seams deliberately torn, my tattered headband,
and 50s glasses, signified to her that I was a byproduct of liberal
60s parents. Nevertheless, she was professional and tended to
my needs. All the names of the various neurological illnesses
looked the same to me and I wondered how medical students could
possibly learn and distinguish this litany of names. I recognized
a few, like meningitis and migraines, on my way to the "p"s, but
they were all so complicated. There was not a lot written about
prosopagnosia, as the writers themselves recognized that this
was a fairly rare brain abnormality. They mentioned that it is a
"misrecognition" process, occurring in the "lateral fusiform gyrus
and posterior superior temporal sulcus where neural activity is
triggered primarily by viewing a human face." So complicated
and esoteric. I had to read this several times, and still did not
comprehend it. The section had several references to Oliver
Sacks and his book, The Man Who Mistook His Wife for a Hat.
I made a mental note to read this book later. Interestingly, the
text also had two pictures of an anonymous individual, one who
is seen normally and the other who is viewed through the gaze
of an individual with prosopagnosia. The face, as seen through
a prosopagnosic gaze, was blurred, like a creepy clown's (I have
attached the pictures on the next page for your observation).
I have a difficult time imagining that Alessandra's face would

appear so horrific to her lover. But, then again, he also suffered from this neurological illness and could only hear and smell her. I would like to hear and smell you myself.

As always,
Adriana

Dear Tessla,

I plan to send these letters that I have written to you soon. Of course, it is very difficult to determine your precise address in Italy. But I am resourceful and will find a way. Don't worry. Today, CineSeen published an article about you, stating that you will be making a foray into American film. How wonderful! But I had discovered you first, as you certainly know from my zeal for you and your brilliant acting. The piece did not specifically mention a film nor the actors with whom you would be working. However, it hinted at your possible attendance at the SoHo International Film Festival. I will certainly be there for a chance to see you as you are, without your numerous facades. I will remain your number one fan for eternity.

We will meet soon,
Adriana

**Cinema Studies 201 — Assigned readings (Excerpt)
Walter Benjamin, The Work of Art in the Age of
Mechanical Reproduction***

"The feeling of strangeness that overcomes the actor
before the camera, as Pirandello describes it, is
basically of the same kind as the estrangement felt
before one's own image in the mirror. But now the
reflected image has become separable, transportable.
And where is it transported? Before the public.
Never for a moment, does the screen actor cease
to be conscious of this fact. While facing the
camera he knows that ultimately he will face the
public, the consumers who constitute the market.
This market, where he offers not only his labor but
also his whole self, his heart and soul, is beyond
his reach. During the shooting he has as little
contact with it as any article made in a factory.
This may contribute to that oppression, that new
anxiety which, according to Pirandello, grips the
actor before the camera. The film responds to the
shriveling of the aura with an artificial build-up
of the 'personality' outside the studio. The cult
of the movie star, fostered by the money of the
film industry, preserves not the unique aura of the
person but the 'spell of the personality,' the phony
spell of a commodity."

---

* Walter Benjamin, "The Work of Art in the Age of
Mechanical Reproduction," in Illuminations: Essays and
Reflections. Schocken Books (New York: 1968). pp. 230-231

TESS RESPONDED MOMENTARILY to the alarming sound of the monitor, indicating that her blood pressure was falling precipitously. In a few short hours, she had been emergently transported to the Intensive Care Unit as she was showing signs and symptoms of septic shock. Her consciousness was continually waxing and waning, and, at times, she was only able to provide half-imparted answers to questions posed to her by the medical staff. At one point, she had thought that Abigail had visited her, her pony-tail moving around effortlessly and her voice, authoritative but gentle. But she did not know if these images had coalesced with her dreams, so that she was instead watching a fictional film sustained by her imagination. She saw fleeting images of faces, hands, and syringes, alternating in slow motion and high speed, a montage sequence that left her visually exhausted. In her state of stupor, she was not sure whether she was alive anymore, save for the pain that she would feel when the medical staff would probe and pinch her to elicit a response in determining whether she was conscious.

The sound of the monitor alerted the nursing staff, as it had Tess. A dopamine drip was started to increase her blood pressure and prevent an acute kidney failure, an inevitability if this decline persisted. Heavy doses of effective antibiotics had already been administered in the ER, but their effect had yet to be realized. It was now known that this patient, Tess, was the same third-year medical student who was rotating in the wards. The nursing and medical staff had given her extra care, as they acknowledged that she was one of them now, that this poor child was undergoing what she had helped others overcome. It was very unfortunate indeed. She had no family that could be notified.

Given the lack of space in the ICU and the limited number of rooms, Tess's room was contiguous with Zamorano's. The rooms were juxtaposed against and resembled one other in architecture and layout, a fact that was not true for the other four. The old man had heard about Tess and inquired extensively about her condition, although, due to privacy concerns, the nurses could provide him with little information. They merely stated that she was in a stable condition and that adequate measures were taken to ensure that her condition would resolve. The staff was surprised that this old man seemed so intent on gathering information on Tess and appeared so alarmed. Zamorano simply replied that she had helped him through his illness and he wished to do so through hers. The gesture was commendable, they thought, quite thoughtful for this patient to care so much for his previous caregiver. The modern medical institution was not concerned about forging such lasting and caring relationships.

Zamorano was feeling better each day and most of his medical problems had resolved. It would probably be only a few days before he was transferred back to the medical floor but, given his propensity for rapid deterioration and unusual presentations, he was to be kept in the ICU as a preventive measure. And he wouldn't have it any other way, given that Tess was in the next room. The old man hoped that he could visit her prior to being transferred to the medical floor. He acknowledged that he cared deeply for this young woman. In fact, he believed that he even loved her.

Cinema Studies 201 — Assigned Readings (Excerpt)
Michel Chion, La voix au cinema*

"So let us define the *screaming point* in a cinematic narrative as something that generally gushes forth from the mouth of a woman, which by the way does not have to be heard, but which above all must fall at an appointed spot, explode at a precise moment, at the crossroads of converging plot lines, at the end of an often convoluted trajectory, but calculated to give this point a maximum impact.... The screaming point is a point of the unthinkable inside the thought, of the indeterminate inside the spoken, of unrepresentability inside representation. It occupies a point in time, but has no duration within. It suspends the time of its possible duration; it's a rip in the fabric of time. This scream embodies a fantasy of the auditory absolute, it is seen to saturate the soundtrack and deafen the listener. It might even be unheard by the screamer."

---

* Michel Chion, <u>La voix au cinema</u> (Paris: Editions de L'Etoile, 1982). p. 68

Dear Tess,

Does anyone else call you Tess? May I transgress this nominal boundary with you? You feel so personal to me, as if I've already met you in another space where we were conspirators together, filming a sordid scene on the Scalinata della Trinita dei Monti in Rome, running down those enormously long and wide staircases as if our lives depended on it, transgressors of the French church, the forerunners of Thelma and Louise. I imagine the wind as our ally, propelling us down farther and farther, until we manage to reach the end of the magnificent steps, having escaped the hungry mob and the papacy. Unlike T. & L., we manage to escape without our deaths. We have eluded death, my dear Tess. But who are you, really? Do you sleep in cotton, silk, or the nude? Cool off with a granita di caffe con panna from the hot midday sun or simply Coke? The hypodermic needle that feeds my visual sensum wants to know whether you partake in your characters' activities. Do you dress up like Francesca and make love like Alessandra? I have had too many hits of this drug called love. I feel that I am close to overdosing. What is the antidote for amor? I'm taking too many hits for you and it's making me delirious and intoxicated.

Voglio vederti stasera,
Adriana

Note: In case you haven't noticed, I've been taking Italian lessons for you. I've also been learning Gaetano Donizetti's L'elisir d'amore (The Elixir of Love) on piano. I hope to perform it for you some day. Tu sei una stella...la mia stella, Tess.

Without Anesthesia

Tess, my dear,

Simulacri, the last of your films, was shown to us at the University
screening room tonight. I must say that although the emotional
force of this film was not as strong as Prosopagnosia's, from a
professional and critical perspective, it outshined all two. I have
never seen acting as complex and jagged as yours. One minute you
are a forlorn wife and the next, a conniving hyena. All believable,
I must say. Bravo, Tess! Bravo! This time, you have upstaged them
all, my dear. The Academy will not forget your performance this
year. To better understand the questions that I would like to pose
for our next class paper, I will attempt to provide a synopsis of
the film (As I've said before, I need to see my thoughts realized
on paper to fully understand them). The diegetic thread concerns
a couple, Bianca (played outstandingly by you) and Antonio, who
lives comfortably in Perugia. He is a banker, she an aspiring
actress. She does not want a normal life. Her relationship with her
husband has become mundane. She loves another. Camillo. Bianca
and Camillo meet for afternoon trysts. A fairly straightforward
plot, one that has been done, again and again. Antonio, however,
is prone to psychodynamic conflicts. He does not trust his wife.
She attempts to push him over the edge with her brilliant acting
while pretending to be an imposter of herself. To try to commit
him to a psychiatric facility and make off with his money. She
tries to make him imagine that an imposter has replaced her. She
cuts her hair differently, not too differently though. Colors her
hair a slightly darker shade of brown. Starts to wear pant suits,
which she did before, but rarely. Similar signs but slightly skewed.
Her speech begins to take on a slight accent, the mannerisms a
bit of ribaldry. Not too severe, though. He begins to notice these
signs, slowly. And when she believes that he may know that she
may not be herself, but another, a simulacra, she resorts back
to her old antics, her old self. A deceitful game of cat and mouse,

this becomes exhausting for him, torturous. She relishes in her coveted role, an actress playing herself who is to be another. At this point, as the psychiatrist in the film purports, Antonio has developed Capgras Syndrome. A syndrome characterized by a sustained delusional belief that a person, closely related to the patient, has been replaced by an imposter. He is soon committed, just as Bianca had planned. And in a twisted reversal of events, because she has played her role so well, she attempts to become the ultimate simulacra, and imitate other famous actresses in her daily course of events. Every week, a new character. Every week, a new lover who loves her for the other person who she is, ad infinitum. Ironically, she, too, develops a misidentification syndrome--a Fregoli Delusion--where she believes that different people are in fact a single person--and is soon committed to the same facility as her husband, Antonio.[*] I admit that the plot was somewhat convoluted for me but your acting, Tess, made it seem like an elementary, linear plot of the first order. Brava! Brava! Bravissima! You deserve a standing ovation and one that I gave to you tonight. The other students were looking at me so strangely, wondering if I myself were not psychotic. They may be right. My life has become tremendously complicated, but also teleological, with you in its midst. They may gaze at me all they want, but their looks will not penetrate me. That I reserve solely for you. Do you feel uncomfortable with my outpourings? I will try to restrain myself.

Always in awe of you,
Adriana

---

* I did a bit of research: Fregoli syndrome is based on the Italian actor, Leopoldo Fregoli (1867-1936), who was so swift in changing his roles on stage, that people thought there was more than one Fregoli. You're his brilliant successor, Tess.

Cinema Studies 201 — Assigned Readings (Excerpt)
Christian Metz, "Disavowal, Fetishism"*

"It is understood that the audience [of a film] is not duped by the diegetic illusion, it 'knows' that the screen presents no more than a fiction. And yet, it is of vital importance for the correct unfolding of the spectacle that this make-believe be scrupulously respected (or else the fiction film is declared 'poorly made'), that everything is set to work to make the deception effective and to give it an air of truth (this is the problem of *verisimilitude*). Any spectator will tell you that he 'doesn't believe it,' but everything happens as if there were nonetheless someone to be deceived, someone who really would 'believe in it.' (I shall say that behind any fiction there is a second fiction: the diegetic events are fictional, that is the first; but everyone pretends to believe that they are true, that is the second; there is even a third: the general refusal to admit that somewhere in oneself one believes that they are genuinely true.)"

---

* Christian Metz, The Imaginary Signifier: Psychoanalysis and the Cinema (Indiana University Press: 1986) p. 813

"LADY TESS, CAN YOU HEAR ME?" She had thought that someone had whispered these words to her, had felt the momentary drift of air that had left this spoken residue. But then Tess had gone back to sleep, having been administered a hypnotic. It had been about six days since she had left the ICU for the medical floor, having safely diverted death after a powerful course of antibiotics, hydration, and perfusion measures. She was also well cared for by the nursing and medical staff which, ultimately, had made a significant impact on her recovery time. The source of the infection was theorized to have been a virulent colony of *E. coli* from a urinary tract infection although the intensivists in the Unit had themselves been surprised from the acute presentation of the sepsis. Nevertheless, they were quite pleased with this young woman's outcome. Their morbidity and mortality statistics would not be jeopardized. The hospital's ranking would remain unchanged.

Tess had progressed quite well over the past few days. Her diet had been changed from pureed to soft food and she was managing her daily activities with the aid of a physical therapist. As the scientific acronyms filled her medical charts, NPO-OOB-ADL, she wondered if they would string together a story, an alphabet, a secret language. Tess had asked the nurses about Zamorano when she had initially regained full consciousness, but was told that he had been discharged during her eventful ICU admission. They remained surprised as to the extent of Tess's relationship with the old man. But they assumed that he had been a very special patient to Tess, one of her first as a medical student. And she would ask the nursing staff, has no one been around to see her then? They would simply smile pleasantly and tell her that the Lord visited her every day. That he had come when no one else had, in those dark nights when war was being waged over her body. Satan had finally relinquished his hold on her because of Him, her daily Visitor. Yes, the Lord had visited her every day and wasn't she the luckiest woman in the world? She had emerged miraculously from this ordeal and she should be thankful to her tireless visitor, they would say.

But Tess knew that she had managed to emerge out of this hole in which she had thrust herself solely through the strength that Zamorano had given her. *He* had been her daily visitor. Continually, in her mind and heart. Even in her sickest of days, she had never lost faith that he would return and see her in the state in which he once were. It was distressing to her, then, that the nurses never mentioned anyone visiting her. She was always vigilant. Her auditory senses would be on guard for the sound of Zamorano's battered cane. Her olfactory senses were vigilant for the pungent smell of which he reeked. She missed these all and was devastated that she would never have a chance to meet her true Savior now, *her* Lord. If he were to appear to her one last time, she would truly do anything for him.

Tess,

I was inspired after viewing Simulacri last night, with you in the
lead role. Today, I purchased and donned a long, wavy black wig in
your remembrance (the black-wigged mannequin was thinking,
she's got an eye on me, this Adriana, as I approached her). So close
to the real. You would have certainly thought that I had shorn
your hair to make this synthetic hairpiece. Monofilament, though,
the best that I could buy, soft to the touch and scalp. The most
difficult were the eyes, purchased at the optometry store next
to Dr. Berezniak's ophthalmology office. "So you want to change
your eye color to blue?" the optometrist had remarked. "No," I
retorted. "I plan to have a new set of eyes altogether." He smirked.
The eyes were certainly the most difficult, placement and all.
I nearly gouged my eyes out for you. I hope that you appreciate
it. I penciled in a black-liner, using a chiseled shading brush to
create a smoky eye. Next, the dress. I headed to the thrift store
near the University and struck gold. The vintage grey suit was
perfect, tailored just right, making my bust and hips look full. I
had become a curvaceous Italian starlet. The fedora hat added the
androgynous element that you, Tess, are so good at. The Jackie
O sunglasses were the finishing touch. Oversized and superfly.
Recalled your role in Rapina perfectly. Why this show? I plan to
become a version of you, my dear Tess, skinned alive. Your role in
Simulacri gave me hope that I could copy you. Yes, you.

Hopeful,
Adriana

Dear Tess,

I was so focused on your face and dress yesterday that I missed
an important part of you. The breasts. Of course. How could I
forget? As the Italians would say, naturale e paffuto. Natural and
plump. How I long to touch them. They exude such confidence,
those D cups. You're so lucky, Tess. My breasts are barely there,
little playthings that look like misshapen walnuts next to your
symmetrical grapefruits. So I looked for some temporary latex
ones. It had to look good. I was to play you today, so I had to
be quick. I headed to some transvestite store that I had seen
around here. I knew I'd find them there. The clerk looked at me
suspiciously, rude. He was black, bearded with gray facial hair,
had an orange wig on with a short green, strapless dress, replete
with a red garter belt, and heavy makeup. He was tall and sinewy,
with correspondingly long legs. Good god, I thought, he looks
like a prostitute from the circus, a complete gender-fuck. This
shop was clearly not tasteful. The latex breasts were organized
on a dirty shelf according to cup size. I had wanted to match the
D cups that you had, but realized that it would be too much for
my gaunt 110 lbs. frame. It would certainly look too fake. I then
grabbed for the last remaining pair of C cups and called myself
lucky to have found them. I wanted to get out of this shit-hole. I
felt so dirty among those paraphernalia. Bras, support hose, wigs,
dildos, all sorts of unclean things. Not your type of store at all. I
paid cash, $22.50, for both breasts, recognizing the poor quality
of the latex. It would do for now. "For your honey?" the black
clerk said at the register, smirking in a not unpleasant manner.
"Of course," I replied, "she is mine and I'm hers." "Lucky lady,"
he retorted, somewhat surprised that I had mentioned a female
lover, while he winked and lasciviously licked his index finger as

if he were picking up a customer. You're not my fucking type, I thought. And what was his type? I scurried out the door.

Your love,
Adriana

THE NURSES WERE WRONG. It wasn't the Lord that visited Tess daily to monitor her progress. Death, herself, managed to make her rounds and quietly stare at this girl. She was fascinated by Tess, knew her secrets as if they were her own, and wanted to see her survive at least a bit longer to see what else she was capable of. Tess's resourcefulness was indubitable. Her oddness fascinated Death, her irregular bangs, the elongated features, her small breasts. Death enjoyed these oddities and had never traded her own disastrous teeth for veneers or the like (although she had whitened them to make her features more striking). As of late, Death had donned the attire of a femme fatale, replete with a fedora hat and veil, vintage Bakelite bangles, a form-fitting dress, black chiffon scarf, and corseted high-heeled pumps. She wore a bright fire-engine red lipstick. It suited her, she thought, brought out her best features: her full lips, her slender, sinewy legs, and striking, white eyes against the black fedora hat and red lips. She would dress this part from now on until she tired of it. Her previous attire consisting of a black robe and scythe, which she had worn for as long as she could remember, was getting tired and had no place in this century. She needed a makeover badly. So she had gone to a movie studio and grabbed what she thought would give her the appearance of a 1940s starlet. Although no one would ever see what she looked like, it still gave her confidence to be as striking and sexy as she thought she could be. It brought another dimension to her lethality, another way to buttress the strength that she, at times, doubted. Yes, Death liked Tess, and did not want her taken away so soon. She was interested to see how this theatrics would progress, how Tess's role would be defined in this human drama.

Without Anesthesia

Tess,

I go from supermarket to supermarket, trying to get noticed for
someone whom I'm not. I linger at the magazine counters, hoping
that someone will approach me and mistake me for you. People
who solicit these counters seem to be waiting for something more,
something to pull them away from their pathetic lives, from their
boredom. I may be one of them. But I continue to wait with no such
luck in this sleepy town of Valhalla, New York. In Norse mythology,
Valhalla is the hall of the slain, ruled over by the God Odin. Maybe
the name will one day suit me if I die for you in combat. I'm here
visiting my parents for Winter break. You'd be pleased to know
that I received an "A" in Cinema Studies 201. The instructor, M.
Vitiello, wrote the most glowing remarks on my last paper for the
class, titled "Mediations of the Real: Simulacri's Simulacra." And
all because of you, Tess. You deserve this honor as much as I. So,
someone does finally approach me in Enter Market on 8 Madison
Ave., as I'm about to exit. I had been at the counter there for close
to an hour reading Harper's Bazaar and Mademoiselle before I had
decided to leave. There wasn't much to choose from. She, a woman
in her late 40s, with cropped dirty brown hair, sporting a Louis
Vuitton purse, not exactly a fashionista, but as close to one as
this town would possibly see, approaches me, and launches into a
monologue. I can't believe the rambling. "Excuse me, Miss. Have I
seen you somewhere before? You look very familiar to me. Perhaps
I've seen you at a restaurant or shop in Manhattan? You really
don't seem to belong in Valhalla. I, myself, am from Manhattan,
picking up my son, Adrien, who just finished his interview for
admittance at New York Medical College. He really is a wonderful
student and I think would make a fantastic doctor. He's sitting
in the car now. Sorry. I must really learn to stop talking. They

call me Chatty Cathy. I'm really sorry to ramble like this." She
really wouldn't let me get a word in. Really talkative, but not quite
annoying enough that I could brush her off. I felt superior though,
thinking that this is my chance to become you, to play a part
that you yourself would've played in Simulacri. So I start in on
the broken Italian that I know, praying that this woman does
not understand nor can she respond to it. "Il mio nome e Tessla.
Sono un attrice in Italia. Forse hai visto Rapina?" That was all I
could muster at that moment, which really took a lot out of me.
I felt the onslaught of a pop quiz that would suddenly turn into
a nightmarish reprisal of a Final (I hadn't received my grade
in Italian 101 yet, and was afraid that I had just scraped by). I
couldn't quite read this woman. She was either looking at me as
if I were a fraud or amazed at seeing such a sophisticated young
Italian woman in an ordinary supermarket here in Valhalla. It
took a while for her to respond, considering the haste at which
she had entered into her initial monologue. I felt safe. The pause
gave me hope. "Oh, I'm afraid I don't understood Italian. But what
a beautiful language it is. All that I understood was that your
name is Tessla. How beautiful! What are the origins? There I go
again. Asking such complicated questions from someone who
barely speaks any English. Excuse me, Miss."

I wanted to abort this conversation as quickly as possible,
but also wanted her to shower me with more compliments. I
decided on the former since this could turn deadly at any moment
and be found out for the fraud that I really was. "Mi dipiace che
non capisco piu l'inglese." This was a phrase with which I was
quite familiar, having substituted the word English for the usual
Italian. It appeared that she had understood me well, and was
retreating from the formidable position of verbal superiority that
she had momentarily held before. "There I go again. Of course, you
didn't understand me. I sometimes don't even understand myself,

dear. You would think that I could easily shed my rural ways about me now that I am 'city folk.' But it's harder than you think. North Dakota is not Manhattan. My true mannerisms come out when I least expect them." So she was acting, too, I thought. We two were actresses in this supermarket called Enter Market. The supermarket's strange name combined with this encounter reminded me of stage directions. Enter stage, Exit stage. I had said my last lines to this woman and was to conclude with this quintessential phrase that didn't need translation, "Arrivederci." As if she had just been initiated into a secret language, the woman, who remained nameless to me, emphatically echoed the same. "Arrivederci, dear. Have a pleasant stay in New York." I exited the supermarket. Exit right. Towards the automatic doors and out onto the backstage where real things happen. I had been you for about ten minutes and felt victorious, envied. I wanted more of this elixir of which I had drunk. I thought that I would turn into a pumpkin, an ordinary girl, Adriana, once I had exited the doors. But, no, the magic continued. I even saw the woman's son in a Toyota Camry parked opposite my car. Adrien, was it? How strange that his name should resemble mine, I thought. So he was to become a doctor. Our lives were so different. But I seductively winked at him for good luck, emphasizing the length of my new eyelashes that I had picked up at a local drugstore. He had been staring at me with his soft and comforting gaze, at my flowing dark locks and curvaceous hips, but turned away after we made eye contact. An Italian starlet getting into a 1991 Honda Civic. How pathetic and fake! I had played the part but had missed a few of the props. The car was one of them.

Loving my new role,
Tess (a.k.a. Adriana)

TO THE AMAZEMENT OF HERSELF and others, Tess had quickly recovered and returned to her duties as a medical student in the hospital. She was assigned another month in the Emergency Department as it allowed her to have more time off without the long term responsibilities of taking care of her own patients. Although her goals were still clear, she had been quite despondent over Zamorano's discharge. She had known that he would eventually leave the hospital, but, in great measure, she had hoped that he would be a prisoner here and even die in this facility. She acknowledged the utter selfishness of such desire, but also acceded that she would be helping others through her actions. She simply needed a mentor who would be beside her at all times, to learn from his illness, and Zamorano had appeared to fill this role quite superbly.

Nevertheless, Tess did what she could to bring herself closer to her patients, to empathize with them. She had undergone one of the most dramatic instances of any disease process, affecting virtually all of her organs. She had developed endocarditis secondary to the infection, acute kidney failure from the lack of perfusion, and hemolysis as a result of a side effect of the antibiotics. Yes, she had experienced a great deal, it was true, but there was so much more to experience, to embody, the mundane symptoms that brought patients to the hospital, those trivial sicknesses that impacted those who suffered from them. She would start with these now until another project presented itself.

In her pathetic apartment room, she did what couldn't be done in the ER. She swallowed any medications that could be stolen from the nurse's cart, simulated non-lethal overdoses, purged herself with syrup of ipecac, and infected her skin while using antibiotics to mitigate its effects. However, nothing compared to the gamble that she had taken with the fecal injection. Nothing came close to the exhilaration and the probability of death that accompanied that gesture. Tess had gambled far too riskily to now resort to petty wagers. She realized that she needed a project that would trump the others. She needed a big win.

T.,

I sometimes like anonymity and having to signify your name
through a capitalized letter initiates us into a secret language. You
could be any person whose name begins with the letter "T": Tara,
Teresa, Tiffany, Tracy. But you are more exotic than that; you are
my Tessla, my Terrific Tessla. Today, I learned about your arrival
into NYC to attend the SoHo International film festival. The film
and culture zine, Screened Out, had a small segment devoted to
what would be your first trip to New York. The editors of the zine
were excited to have you here, in the City, as they were partially
responsible for your success. They had promoted you, it was true,
but you would've found stardom sooner or later. It was bound to
happen. They mentioned that you would be featured in their next
month's issue devoted to the New International Cinema, featuring
the directors Abbas Kiarostami, Tom Tykwer, and Kar Wai Wong,
among others. You would be here in eight days. Just in time for the
first day of screening. It was unclear which of your films would be
featured (Rapina, Prosopagnosia, Simulacri). But this unknown
excited me more, like a child that is hard-pressed to guess the
mystery awaiting her in a Kinder Surprise egg. As a side note, an
old childhood friend had once brought me such a chocolate egg
from a trip to Germany, which made me realize the force of such a
surprise. What would I find inside? A diamond ring, a miniature
globe of the world, gold coins? But my hopes were trashed when
all I retrieved was a lousy, fake, plastic watch, non-functional
and orange. I had not liked the toy, but immensely enjoyed the
prospect of finding something unearthly hidden beneath the
hollow chocolate. So, yes, whatever the film may be, I will enjoy
guessing whom you will be onscreen. I am planning to purchase
a ticket for the show and am ABSOLUTELY THRILLED that I will
have an opportunity to see you in the flesh. No simulacra. I will be
counting the days, T.

Yours,
a. (uncapitalized -- I am so much less significant than you)

Dear Tess,

Having arrived in Manhattan today for the SoHo International
Film Festival, I felt like Pinocchio leaving Geppetto for Calzoni's
Carnival. I felt alive. No longer puppet, I was in complete control
of my destiny. I chanced upon the first hotel on St. Mark's Place
in the East Village that appeared to be within my budget. I knew
what I would be getting, as the very façade of the hotel hinted at
the spartan and decrepit condition awaiting me. After I checked
in, I went upstairs to Room 1111, to drop off my small suitcase
and roam the city. I momentarily thought it odd that the second
floor should have a room labeled 1111, but then my thought veered
towards you and I left the hotel. Like Pinocchio, I was sure to
meet some temptations and the thought excited me. I was still
dressed as you and my skin was not so ready to have your aura
stripped from it. I was continuously adjusting my black, wavy wig
as I walked. It was a bit annoying, but at least my scalp was not
itching. The monofilament had been a wise choice.

Fun City Cappuccino & Tattoo at 94 St. Mark's Place was
the first place that caught my eye as I walked. I have never done
such a thing. Never have I been so spontaneous as to walk into a
tattoo parlor, not knowing what to expect. You have injected that
hypodermic needle of love into my veins and it burns. It burns
so badly. I hoped that your name would be forever emblazoned
on my skin. Acting like you, made me want to be you and labeled
as you. The tattoo appeared to be the perfect progression. I
contemplated an image of a heart rising from the ashes, Phoenix-
like, but ultimately knew that the etching should be completely
of you. Your image in words. Cursive, because you brought
to mind an older, classical era where Italian starlets ruled.
The tattoo artist approached me and, like the Tessla Ferrara
whom I was emulating, I asked him for such a design. I tired to

speak broken English to emulate you, but it was difficult. There certainly was no way I could communicate my ideas in Italian. I improvised. He bought the act. He hadn't heard of Tess before (I had truncated your name for the design, as it felt more personal). I told him that it was Italian. He offered me cappuccino. I sipped the warm libation, thinking that its magic-producing effects would momentarily transform me. I was already in a magic shop, I thought, and my most heroic trick would be to disappear from myself and completely become you. The tattooist drew a preliminary copy of what was to be etched on my skin and revealed it to me:

I thought it beautiful. It reminded me of Tess of the d'Urbervilles, the lettering very proper and Victorian. He asked how conspicuous I wanted this tattoo to be. I didn't want others to really know our secret, so I told him that he could etch the design on the back of my neck. The nape is a sensitive area of the body, Tess. It is seductive and strong at the same time. It was appropriate for us. The etching hurt a bit but the pain made me realize that this was real. That my love for you would not die. I'll have you emblazoned on my skin forever.

Love,

Tess

Tess,

I'm counting the days to our meeting. Four to go now. The three days here in Manhattan have been bliss, with you obsessively in my thoughts. I plan to present this collection of letters to you, as a memento, as a souvenir of what we have forged together. I'm sure you will find them worthy of you and a pleasure to read. I have tied them with a black ribbon, resembling the headband that you wore as a Jackie O in Rapina. I have also scented the letters with my fragrance, Christian Dior's Poison, redolent of a heady cocktail of coriander, vetiver, and heliotrope. Musky, but sweet. Don't worry. I don't intend to poison you, my dear. Far from it. I've typewritten all of these letters since my writing can be illegible at times. Should I have translated them as well? I thought about this but decided against it. (The original is so much better, although, I must admit, fake can be just as good as you have demonstrated time and time again in your acting.) The magazines all say that your English is quite good as you were schooled in London for some time. Nevertheless, I have purchased an English to Italian dictionary for those words and phrases that may seem out of reach. I am hoping that not too many of my words and thoughts will be "lost in translation," as they say. But how do I give you this prized collection? I inquired about the place of accommodation for those invited to the film festival, and was told by a source at the University--the editor of the film department's student-run journal, Reel--that most would be staying at the Waldorf Astoria Hotel on Park Avenue. I should say that you have really moved up in the ranks, Tess. As I've been told, the Waldorf is one of the most opulent, classical hotels in all of Manhattan. I think that I'll drop them off at the front desk. If you receive them and are now holding the letters in your hand, my mission was successful.

Always resourceful,
Adriana

P.S. I would be grateful if you could offer me an interview for our University's film journal, Reel, while you're in Manhattan. Gamble Swart, the editor of the journal, gave me free reign to conduct it in whatever manner I choose. Please name a time and place where we could meet after your premiere. I am utterly excited that we can have a chance to talk alone, my dear Tess. You mean the world to me.

KNOW THAT YOU CAN'T GO ON LIVING ANOTHER FUCKING DAY, BUT KNOW THAT YOU'LL DO IT ANYWAY. IT'S EASIER NOT TO MAKE A CHOICE. A CHOICE INVOLVES ENERGY, WHICH YOU DON'T HAVE. GET DRESSED. LEAVE YOUR CESSPOOL OF AN APARTMENT. DON'T MAKE EYE CONTACT OR TALK TO YOUR NEIGHBORS, THE METH ADDICTS NEXT DOOR, BECAUSE THEY CAN MAKE TROUBLE FOR YOU, SOMETHING THAT YOU CAN'T AFFORD. GET TO THE HOSPITAL WHERE YOU'VE BEEN ROTATING FOR THE PAST SEVERAL MONTHS. SMILE AT THE PATIENTS BECAUSE YOU HAVE TO, BECAUSE THEY EXPECT YOU TO. SAY HELLO TO THE NURSING STAFF. PRETEND THAT YOU DON'T KNOW THAT THEY'RE TALKING ABOUT YOU, TALKING ABOUT THE MEDICAL STUDENT WHOSE APPEARANCE IS SO STRANGE, BUT WHOM THEY PITY BECAUSE, GOD, SHE JUST UNDERWENT SUCH A HORRIBLE ORDEAL AND SHE ALMOST DIED. DON'T LET THE PITY GET TO YOU AND, IF IT DOES, YOU CAN'T DO ANYTHING ABOUT IT ANYWAY BECAUSE IT TAKES ENERGY TO MAKE A CHOICE AND YOU JUST DON'T HAVE ANYTHING LEFT IN YOU ANYMORE. RECOGNIZE THAT YOU WERE DOING THIS FOR THE PATIENTS, FOR THE OLD MAN, WHO HAS HAD SUCH A HOLD ON YOU, AND YOU REALLY CAN'T IMAGINE LIVING WITHOUT HIM. KNOW THAT YOU'RE SEVERELY DEPRESSED, AND YOU MISS THE OLD MAN'S PUNGENT SMELL THAT REMINDS YOU SO MUCH OF THE OLD CHURCHES IN ROME, AND YOU MIGHT AS WELL KILL YOURSELF, AND YOU WOULD IF YOU HAD MORE ENERGY AND HAD ACCOMPLISHED YOUR GOAL, THIS GOAL THAT HAS BEEN THRUST UPON YOU. THERE'S A PATIENT WITH A SEIZURE IN ROOM 4. OPEN THE DOOR. GREET THE PATIENT. INTRODUCE YOURSELF, EVEN IF YOU REALLY WANT TO BE FUCKING DEAD NOW AND WOULD BE IF YOU JUST HAD THE GOD DAMN ENERGY AND HAD ACCOMPLISHED YOUR GOAL.

IT WAS NOT DRAMATIC. A routine, generalized seizure in Room 4, the same room in which she had found herself several months ago as a patient with an impending septic shock. She traced her steps to that room as someone who knew how many steps were needed to open the door, as to what to expect once inside. The same gurney in which she herself had lain as a patient with the same starched white sheets that were so abrasive to the touch. She knew, too, the dialogue that was expected of her once there. Nothing to set herself apart from another medical student, except her name: "Hello. My name is Tess, a 3rd year medical student who will be taking your history and conducting a physical exam." It was all so pathetic, really. She had found herself more depressed than ever, on the verge of a neurotic breakdown. It was not the sort of depression that she had encountered when she first came to this new town, as a transferee to this medical school. She had anticipated feeling depressed in this place, a situational depression that usually went away with routine, with banal familiarization. But this was different. This was a feeling that wrenched her guts, disemboweled her, and left her empty and so dead inside. She had not seen her mother in over a year, when she had suddenly decided to transfer here from her medical school in New York. Her father was long dead. She realized that she did not miss him at all, that his heart attack had really been a death wish. She had wished so on her tenth birthday, blown out her last candle with all of her breath to make sure that this wish could be granted. It was. Eight years later.

So as not to wither away and accomplish what she had set out to do, she took refuge in her projects. One of these would probably be the death of her, she thought. It was certainly a possibility. Her nearly three-week hospital stay was a reminder of that. She had purposely suppressed these thoughts. Her death would have to be the last gesture, after she had experienced all that she possibly could. Her extreme suffering disturbed her. It burned so much, this desire to feel the pain of humanity as if it were her own pain and illness. She imagined herself as a vampiress who merely lives through the sickness and blood of others. She was an addict. Hit after hit, she needed more. Her supply was running dangerously low.

The seizure in Room 4 may not have been dramatic enough for Tess. She walked in the room with her languid pace. Her expression was lugubrious, her eyes, downcast. Gone were the zeal and fervor of when she had first encountered patients. She looked up. And she thought that she saw the face of the Lord. Could this be really possible, she thought? Who had brought him to her? Was the Lord really forgiving her for abandoning Him at such a young age, for the shameful decisions that she had made?

Zamorano was gazing at her, his hair longer and whiter than ever. He had grown a beard as well. He looked biblical. Yes, Tess, thought, maybe this was the Lord himself, coming down in the form of man to acknowledge and congratulate her for what she had strived to accomplish, for her utter anguish to better humanity through self-destructing herself. It made perfect sense to her.

Tess did not avert her gaze this time, as she had done in times past. The angle was direct. It was forthcoming. Zamorano noticed this as well and smiled. "My dear Lady Tess. Never would I have imagined seeing your lovely face after these months. I see that you are healed completely. I would have liked to visit you, but I was discharged so soon after. That is no excuse, really, but I could not bear the thought that you were so sick and that you might die. I am so pleased that you are alive."

Tess was at a loss of words. Zamorano's monologue was exactly what she had wanted to hear. She had rehearsed his lines in her mind repeatedly so as to form a response to them. Due to the unimaginable circumstance in which she now found herself, she could utter no words. But her silence conveyed so much more to the old man.

"I see that you are very surprised to see me, Lady Tess," Zamorano continued. "I, too, never thought that I would return here. You, Tess, are the magnet that has such a gravitational pull on me. You can perhaps say that this has been my destiny. To see you one last time before I perish from this earth."

"Oh, Mr. Zamorano, please don't say such things," she quickly responded. The entire hospital cares for you so much. You are practically family here." She smiled briefly. "Although I am quite sad that you are here again, I am comforted that I'm able to see you again. We will try to determine the nature of your seizures. It appears that you've had several episodes today. The Ativan seems to have controlled them for the time being. I'll suggest to the Attending that we order several tests. We'll start with a head CT and go on from there. I'll have you under my personal guidance. Don't you worry."

He really loved her, he thought. He was sure of that now. He watched her leave the cold room with a determination and fortitude that he had not previously seen.

Dear Tess,

I am now certain that you are staying at the Waldorf so I attempt
to drop off my collection of letters at the front desk, just as I
had planned. As I enter this opulent hotel, I feel fake amidst
the Italian travertine and oiled veneer, stooping a bit, my eyes
slightly downcast. But then I remember that I am still reenacting
you, made up in the same garb, with the same wig, eyes, and
clothes that I had used in the supermarket. My posture suddenly
becomes erect, my face a little more concentrated and serious, as I
emphasize my curvature with the Italian stilettos that I had also
purchased at the vintage store. I think that I forgot to mention the
shoes last time. A fairly beat-up Ferragamo, but, nevertheless, star
quality, befitting you. You must remember: I am playing the part
of the Italian starlet that is you.

    I ask the clerk, an older gentleman with a stern jaw but
kind eyes, in Italian mind you, that I'm an old friend of yours,
a Manhattan transplant from Rome, who has come to visit you
after all of these years. I start with Italian and plan to regress
to English once he tells me that he can't speak or understand
the former: "Sono un vecchio amica di Tessla Ferrara, che e ora
vive a Manhattan." To my chagrin and utter horror, however,
he responds in Italian, one that seems authentic and too fast for
me to fully comprehend. "Che bella sorpresa! Sigra. Ferrara sara
lieto di vedervi." I remain frozen, barely comprehending what he
has said to me. Something about a "lovely surprise," I think, and
"happiness." I never expected this. How foolish to think that I
could act as a foreigner in this international hotel. I, nevertheless,
try to gauge his tone at the moment. Yes, kind eyes. But a stern
jaw. Has he found me out? I try to recover my losses and quickly
retreat. I think that I've been found out. I smile demurely, as

you would've done, and bat my lashes. I think that even an old gentleman like he couldn't resist an Italian starlet, fake as she may be. My last words to him before I fully pounce out the heavy rotating doors and one that I had rehearsed numerous times: "Potrebbe dare a queste lettere Ms. Ferrara?" as I hand him the letters. I had rehearsed much more to tell him in Italian, to show off, but, at that moment, it was a miracle that I was able to vocalize these few spoken words. "Naturalmente cari, " he retorted, as the scent of the Poisoned letters wafted past me. My initial success at the supermarket was tempered with this bitter loss. I had failed my screen test, but, most importantly, failed you, my dear Tess.

Still only a novice actress,
Adriana

FUCK YOU, FUCK YOU, FUCK YOU, tess,

Do you really mean to neglect me? I'm on the verge of a fucking breakdown and I've drunk too much of this love potion to go on living without you. This is the shit I found myself in: So I return to the Waldorf on the day of your screening to inquire about the letters that I had given to the clerk to give to you. I was certain that you had received the letters at this point but was obsessing about them nonetheless. I was still acting the part of Tessla Ferrara but was now more impeccably dressed, albeit with the same wavy black wig, blue eyes, and heavy latex breasts (the eyes were more defined, Egyptian-like, as I had used a thicker shade of black eyeliner). I had returned to the vintage clothing store and purchased a stunning, black knit, wrap dress, reminiscent of '70s von Furstenberg. Very classic, very Italian. The price was a little steep, but the dress was perfect for my purpose. I think you had worn such an outfit as Alessandra, in a scene where you had spontaneously stripped off your dress and your lover began to go down on you and fuck you like the animal you are. (I know I have atavistically regressed into this crude language, but can you really blame me?) I'm certain that you remember the scene, Tess. I think you had rather enjoyed the fucking, and then I saw that black dress lying on a heap on the motel floor, mixed in with your lover's stained jeans and torn dress shirt, having denigrated into nothingness. I plan to resurrect this black dress for what it had been before, before you had stripped it off. This is my homage to it.

I glanced around this pristine castle of a hotel to see whether the clerk to whom I had given the letters was present. He was not. He had been substituted during the day by a handsome, considerably younger-looking gentleman, with deep blue eyes that shined quite brilliantly even from a distance. I could not read him

nor did I dare after my last encounter with the clerk whom I had
first met here. I assumed that this gentleman could speak Italian
and was prepared for a hasty retreat once I had determined the
status of the letters. He was eyeing me as I approached him, his
short brown hair carefully and impeccably brushed to the side
with a small amount of gel. He was the model of a hotel employee,
groomed perfectly and proper in his decorum. I wondered if he
were acting this part that he was assumed to play or whether this
was his normal demeanor. He seemed genuine. I began to prepare
for a small battle.

As I finally reached the desk, I realized that his bluest eyes
were no more real than mine. Having now worn these colored
contacts for you, Tess, having changed my eyes, I could now also
detect deception in others'. He noticed the same in mine but my
gaze overpowered his, signaling to him that he was acting the
role of a hotel clerk at this international hotel. This clerk's eyes
were his Achilles' heel, as he let his guard down, realizing that
I had taken him for whom he was. I felt confident now, realizing
that our outward deceptions had actually made us confidantes,
that this deception had somehow brought us together and would
keep us so. When he looked down, I knew I had won this battle.
Basking in confidence, I started: "Buongiorno, signore. Ho
lasciato una serie di lettered da dare al Ms. Ferrara. Forse lei li
ricevono?" I had rehearsed this phrase too well and it played out
much better with this new found confidence. The once formidable
clerk looked pathetic. His expression, timidly quizzical, his voice,
slightly trembling and cautious. "I am sorry, Miss, but I do not
speak Italian. Do you perhaps speak a bit of English?" I had won
him over as the fake Italian starlet whom I was. I replied: "Oh
pardon me, Sir. I do speak a little English. I am a friend of Ms.
Tessla Ferrara who is staying in your hotel. I dropped off a set of

letters for her three days ago and gave them to the other clerk. Has she received them yet?" As I was speaking my native English, I realized that it would need to sound bastardized, with a bit of an accent thrown in. I was not so good at this yet, but was trying to speak slowly and use simple English, without any specific idioms that could give me away as a native. I was trying to change my sentence structure around, as some Italians do when speaking English, but I had not mastered the art of foreign dialogue yet.

He briefly looked around his desk and picked up the collection of letters that were meant for you. It were as if my heart had stopped at that moment and that potion of love of which I had drunk had congealed to black, sticky filth. I was instantly outraged at the clerk who was meant to give these letters to you, never thinking that you had refused them. So, without thinking, my obnoxious American English simmered through and the act of a sophisticated Italian starlet went to shit. "What do you mean she never received them?" I shouted. "I gave that other clerk full instructions to give those letters to Tessla. She must get those letters." I realized then that although I had won the battle, this clerk, the one with the fake-blue eyes pretending to be a paragon employee of the Waldorf, had decimated me in war.

He hesitated for a moment before he went on, fully cognizant that I had lost my cool in this screen test. As the gentleman whom he pretended to be, he never let on that he had witnessed my debacle in front of a one-person audience. "I am extremely sorry, but Ms. Ferrara told us to dispense of these letters after she looked at them. She thought that they were the work of a stalker and instructed us not to accept anything else from you. We have kept these letters here, realizing that you may come back and collect them. After all, they look beautifully packaged and the scent is extraordinary. The letters certainly do not belong in the rubbish.

She also told us to contact security if you were to return. I really don't think that's necessary. I think she may have misunderstood your intentions."

I didn't know how to respond, but realizing that my act was over, I tried to salvage what I could, offer my thanks in English, retrieve the letters, and push out of those heavy rotating doors into the chilly December sky. The world was dead to me at that moment and so were you, Tess. Those letters should really have been poisoned for you.

You're so dead to me,
Adriana

By the way: After some brief investigation, I learned that your real name is Maria Rossi. How fucking pathetic! Nevertheless, to me, you're still the bastardized Tess whom I know so well now.

OPEN THE GILDED DOORS OF THE WALDORF ASTORIA. WALK INTO THE LOBBY OF THE HOTEL. REALIZE THAT YOU CAN'T BELIEVE THAT YOU'RE REALLY HERE, THAT YOU'VE FINALLY MADE IT, THAT YOU'RE A BONAFIDE MOVIE STAR. THE HOTEL CLERK WILL GREET YOU WITH A WARM "BUONA SERA." YOU CAN'T DECIDE HOW YOU WANT TO BE PERCEIVED BY THESE PEOPLE, YOUR AUDIENCE. RESOLVE THAT YOU SHOULD ACT AS A FILM STAR IN THE U.S. WOULD: COLD AND DISTANT, ALTHOUGH YOU'RE ACTUALLY HUMBLE UNDERNEATH ALL THOSE LAYERS, YOUR DEFENSE MECHANISMS. THE CLERK WILL HAND YOU LETTERS OF AN INTOXICATING SCENT. RECOGNIZE THAT THE SCENT IS OF YOUR FAVORITE PERFUME, CHRISTIAN DIOR'S POISON. LOOK OVER THESE LETTERS. UNDERSTAND THAT YOUR BIGGEST FAN WROTE THEM. DON'T SHOW INTEREST IN THESE LETTERS OR ACKNOWLEDGE THEIR SINCERITY BECAUSE, TO DO SO, WOULD SHOW YOUR WEAKNESS AND EXPOSE THAT YOU'RE REALLY NOT A MOVIE STAR BECAUSE WHAT MOVIE STAR WOULD BE SO EXCITED ABOUT LETTERS FROM A FAN? RECOGNIZE THAT IF THIS GIRL WHO WROTE THESE LETTERS WERE HERE AND YOU WERE NOT A MOVIE STAR, YOU WOULD EMBRACE HER BECAUSE NO ONE SHOWS YOU TRUE LOVE ANYMORE AND THIS GIRL TRULY CARES FOR YOU LIKE NO ONE ELSE GENUINELY HAS IN A LONG TIME. ACT AS YOU THINK A FILM STAR WOULD. TELL THE CLERK THAT THE GIRL WHO WROTE THESE LETTERS IS A STALKER, AND THAT HE SHOULD NOTIFY SECURITY IF SHE WERE TO RETURN. TOUCH YOUR SHORTENED BLONDE HAIR, WHICH YOU RECENTLY CUT AND COLORED. RECOGNIZE THAT, UNDERNEATH IT ALL, YOU'RE STILL MARIA ROSSI, THE ITALIAN WITH HUMBLE ORIGINS FROM A SMALL MEDIEVAL TOWN IN ITALY, CASTELSARDO. BUT TOUCH YOUR SHORTENED BLONDE HAIR AGAIN. REALIZE THAT YOU DON'T REALLY KNOW WHO

YOU ARE ANYMORE, HAVING PLAYED ROLES THAT REQUIRE YOU TO THINK THAT YOU CAN'T RECOGNIZE FACES, THAT YOU ARE DYING FROM A PRION DISEASE, THAT YOU THINK YOU ARE OTHER ACTRESSES IN YOUR FILM. DON'T LET ON THAT YOU'VE NEVER NOT BEEN A MOVIE STAR BECAUSE THIS IS THE ROLE THAT YOU'VE NOW ASSUMED AND YOU BETTER KEEP ON PLAYING IT.

Scene: 3 A.M. Hospital Room 204. Door closed. Minimalist, hospital décor. Flickering lights. Zamorano sitting up in a plush hospital Cadillac chair, somewhat disheveled, his hospital gown loosely tied in the back. Subdued voices of the hospital staff resonate in the background. Zamorano holds an insulin-filled syringe and is in the process of injecting himself. Tess suddenly opens the door and surprises him. He throws the syringe on the floor.

Zamorano: (Surprised, but composed. Stutters a bit) My dear Lady Tess. You caught me unawares. It is very nice of you to visit me so frequently. I do relish our time together. You have been a true beacon guiding a forlorn ship.

Tess: (After a protracted silence, dismayed and unable to answer): Mr. Zamorano, it's a relief to know that your seizures have stopped for the time being.

Zamorano: Yes, I'm thankful for that as well. To have no control of one's body, that is agony.

Tess: The results of our tests have confirmed that you don't harbor an insulinoma, a tumor in the pancreas, which is what we initially thought. This is certainly good news. We determined this by checking a C-peptide level that tells us whether the insulin is coming from your pancreas or if it's artificial. It appears that (after a moment of hesitation) you have been injecting yourself and (hesitation) causing your own seizures.

Zamorano: (Again, a brief period of silence and Zamorano is tremulous): How can I deceive you now, my dear, when you come out with your earnest accusations? I'm afraid that you're correct, Tess. And, having seen the syringe fall from my hand, you now have the evidence as well.

Tess: I don't know what to say, Mr. Zamorano (she is on the verge of tears). But why? Why? You don't know how much I've cared for you and still care for you (Tess is crying hysterically now). I cannot…

Zamorano (Hesitant to speak): Tess. You must believe me, my dear. I have not meant to deceive you. That's the last thing that I ever wanted. To see you hurt like this. I have never cared for anyone else like I have you. I…I love you, Tess.

Tess: (Crying even more loudly now, tears dripping from her nostrils) Please don't say those words. Not when I'm so confused. I suppose that all those other illnesses…they were the same. You've deceived me, when all that I ever wanted to do was to understand you better. Oh, God. Oh, God. What have I done to myself? (One hears a scream from Tess and then more crying)

Zamorano: (Standing up from his chair and walking to Tess, placing his hands on her cheeks) You don't know what I've gone through, Tess. And to think that I've hurt you intentionally. I might as well kill myself. All I ever wanted… for someone to love me, adore me for myself. But it was always through my sickness that I was ever loved. You, too, loved me for my sickness, didn't you?

Tess: (Somewhat composing herself, but still sniffling) I might have before, but now…

(Lights flicker and all turns dark)

Fragments of Damaged Life:
The Collected Papers of Anton Gadomsky*
(Excerpt)

I contemplate what to do next. This alley is such a dead space, the perfect place for me, for one who is destitute, a runaway. I wonder whether this has always been my nature or something that has been cast upon me. Fate, perhaps. I am a traveling performer, an actor who gives his heart and soul, and doesn't ask much for return. Mother would have been proud. My acting abilities far surpass hers now. I'm a Maximilian Schell to her Minto Cato.

I think about my other family, the Goldman's, (rest their souls) from whom I've learned compassion and goodness. I contemplate the deceptions that I've forced upon them. They had believed me all along. My ersatz father, the doctor, couldn't see past my childhood illnesses. They were all so real to him. This was 54 years ago. I am still the same actor, disguised in different personas and costumes.

Completely alone, but completely free. There is nothing to bind me to anyone. Except this dagger in which I hold in my hand. There is so much tainted history here. Its handle, so abrasive to the touch. This is perfect, I think. Although I have carried it with me all these years, I have never once thought that it was truly a part of me.

I envision myself as a samurai, committing seppuku, in front of spectators. I am cloaked in the purest and whitest of kimonos. Unlike Mother in black face, my face is ghastly white. I raise my dagger. I plunge it into my abdomen. A left-to-right cut, a disembowelment. I realize, however, that I don't wish to kill myself. I simply want to perform. I want to play this sick role. It's always

* Edited and Foreword by Daniel Rubenstein, M.D., <u>Fragments of Damaged Life: The Collected Papers of Anton Gadomsky</u> Prometheus Press (Los Angeles: 1999)

the sick role.

I find a place in the alley that is completely desolate. It is not so difficult here, in Omaha. I take the dagger in my right hand and stab myself in the abdomen, left lower quadrant. I make sure to avoid the small intestine and aim lower for the colon. The wound widens. The blood flows. I writhe in pain.

I now attempt to find an area in the alley where passersby roam. A quick left and I encounter a young couple, hand-in-hand, to whom I run. "Please help me—I've been stabbed," I cry timidly, while gasping for air. I am bleeding profusely now, but my adrenaline and endorphins are no match for it, this red liquid that is my life force. My acting trumps it. I fall to the ground, truly exhausted now. I have given all I can, a fairly respectable performance. The couple is aghast and motionless for a few seconds. In a moment, the young man runs into the streets to find a phone booth. He stumbles upon a police officer instead. I am transported to the emergency room-—then into the operating room. I open my eyes in Recovery, with a plastic pouch sown [*sic*] on my abdomen. The surface of my body now functions as an anus. I have been colostomized. Shit now runs onto me.

t.,

Are you surprised? Yes, I'm still writing these letters to you and
you may in fact want to read them again. Soon. I am not divulging
those plans to you yet. We must return to the day in which you
stabbed me in the heart. As close to literal as it could get without
your having committed the act. I returned to the hotel in which
I was staying for the week that you would be in town. Not the
Waldorf by any stretch. I had wasted my savings on you. I had
lied to my parents and had told them that I was attending a week-
long film seminar at the University. They trusted me implicitly. I
obviously question my judgment now. It has been so skewed by you
in my midst.

   When I returned to the hotel, I was a complete mess,
completely fucked-up. The attendant at the desk was a twenty-
some year old boy, with greasy hair and old acne scars, who was
busy reading a comic book. He was befitting this hotel and my
place in the universe at this moment. I felt removed from my body,
floating in air, having automatically retraced my steps back. If
you feel any sympathy for me, please spare your tears for the next
person who may die. I know you're an ice-cold bitch. You have
demonstrated as much.

   The boy looked up from his comic book and quickly glanced
at me. I made no eye contact. I said nothing to him. I had my
key with me, but I felt his unobtrusive gaze as it followed me
upstairs. Room 1111 on the second floor. It felt that my universe
was in complete disarray. 11:11. I wished that you were dead at
that moment, that you had drunk of those poisoned letters. I was
clutching that collection of letters, the loose Jackie O headband
barely keeping them in place. The smell of the Poison had
definitely waned but a waft of the coriander soothed my nostrils

and made the smell of this antiquated room more pleasant. The Poison brought back memories of my teenage years living in Valhalla with my brother and parents. I received this fragrance first as a Christmas gift on my 16th birthday when my mother noticed that it may help my relationship with boys. It didn't. I appeared strange to these boys, as someone absorbing herself in old, silent films like Metropolis and The Cabinet of Dr. Caligari, movies that transported me either to a future or a past that was severed from any reality that I was living. Although the boys didn't ridicule me, being fairly attractive for someone they felt to be so strange, they didn't befriend me either. I didn't mind, as I was in my own hermetic bubble that kept me safe and distant from everyone. As I was reminiscing about the past that was no longer, I realized that I didn't need these words that were written to you, these letters that had somehow solidified our relationship. You obviously didn't. What a callous bitch you are, Tessla. I grabbed some matches that were lying on the bedside table, flimsy ones that one could barely light, and attempted to start a fire, a conflagration, to burn those letters, burn you, out of my fucking mind. No one had ever hurt me so. Once the matches were lit, a tremor invaded my hands as I then tried to hold the letters. I lit the edges and, no sooner had I done so, I realized that the papers could be used as evidence to acquit me from the crime I was to commit. No one would indict a forlorn lover. Everyone understands a love that has been maliciously poisoned. Instantaneously, I threw the letters on the floor and began to stamp the fire out. It worked. Save the burned edges, the letters were saved. You, Tessla, may have the pleasure of following me into heaven or hell. I will be seeing you tonight at the premiere.

Forsaken, but not to be forgotten,
Adriana

Tess,

I'm through with you. Through. Nevertheless, I wait outside the
Film Forum on Houston St. to await your premiere. I am smoking
Marlboro Menthols, one cigarette after another, to mitigate the
nervousness I feel in your midst. Don't get me wrong. I hate you
for the ice-cold bitch that you are and would like to see you dead.
But I have to determine the depth of your coldness, the cruelty
that you beget. I don't believe that you could see me, without
feeling remorse for what you've done. Ultimately, I think this has
all been a mistake. That the message was somehow not decoded
properly, that you misunderstood the letters. I did say that things
get lost in translation, didn't I? It's my fault. I know. Thus I wait
outside to read your eyes. There is no way to misread eyes. That's
why I stand out here in this bitter, December cold. To see the
hard evidence. I hear a nearby conversation: tickets cannot be
purchased to your premiere. It is a closed list, comprised of the
industry and media elite. I budge my way into security, pretending
to be a film critic from an Italian journal. I feel confident in my
Italian. I've had too many dress rehearsals not to.
 I start in with one of the security guards. I still look as you.
I'm hoping that he doesn't think this is all a practical joke. I do
what Jackie O would do. Remove the first thing that she would
see in the mirror before leaving home. I have no mirror. I instead
feel my face and remove the first object. The Jackie O, superfly
sunglasses. How ironic. I change my name and begin my lines.
"My name is Alesssandra and I'm a critic for Reel, an Italian film
journal. I'm here to cover the film." I know he won't understand
so I switch to English. It seems believable. But he points to the
list and nonchalantly replies, "I'm sorry. You're not on the list."
I've gone too far to let this little obstacle deter me. I'm a bit angry

now and my Italian takes over. He cannot understand me. But I
see that he doesn't want a scene, so he motions me inside. I feel a
minor triumph. I've slipped through the cracks. Gained entrance
into heaven through hard work. Mocked salvation.

Having learned from the best,
Adriana

Cheap t.,

My pupils adjust too fast from the white of the December sky
to this dark, cinematic space. Plato's cave comes to mind. I
momentarily feel around for guidance. Am I walking into a trap
designed by you? The thought crosses my mind. Your role as
the conniving Bianca was too real. You may be luring me at this
moment. I've begun to forget what a brilliant actress you are. The
thought that I've been played somehow comforts me. Maybe I've
misunderstood. This has been a way to gauge my reaction. Your
screen test for me to see if I've performed to your standards, if
I can act beside you in your next film. Once my pupils acclimate
to this artificial night, I reach for the first seat that is available
to me. I plan to scan you from afar. A bird's eye view of the entire
event. A God hovering above you. A Muybridge and Lumiere,
dissecting your minute movements, subjecting you to cuts,
playbacks, and slow-mos. I plan to archive my film of you in my
brain, to edit as I please. I glimpse around, like the bird that I am,
to capture you. My head as movie camera, the tattooed nape as a
rotating stand. You are nowhere to be seen. I zoom in on a space
of increased activity. My eyes have a difficult time recording and
filtering the light of the camera flashes. But the flashes soften. I
begin recording. There you are. I didn't imagine it like this. You
have dyed your hair a shade of blonde and cut your hair. The
makeup has intensified as well. You appear completely changed,
completely modified. The old Tessla doesn't exist anymore. I'm
now the copy that has supplanted the original. It takes a while for
me to take this in. This is unexpected, not what was rehearsed.
You sit at least twenty feet from me, but my eyes have become
super sharp in the interim, a super-crafted lens whose focus
is unparalleled. You are clinging to the arms of a handsome

gentleman. His hair is gray, shorn, and sophisticated. He's comfortable with himself and it shows. You, Tess, are a fucking wreck by comparison. You need adoration, a blonde-blackhead, who has cheapened herself in the process. Your eyes are soulless, disconnected. I can now see that you care nothing for me. I'm a better version of you, my dear, and you should be lucky that I have preserved you. Having recorded you, I rush out of the movie theater, realizing that you will be subject to heavy editing. The possibilities are endless.

You should be sorry,
The editor

t.,

As I hastily leave the Film Forum, I realize that spectators are mistaking me for you; they're photographing me. They don't realize that, in the interim, you have recklessly managed to transform yourself to a cheap blonde. I, by comparison, am the sophisticated Italian starlet whom you once embodied. I cannot help but to smile. And then I hear a person in the crowd saying to others that I'm not the real Tessla, that you no longer look like I do. Your aura still surrounds me, however, as I dart into the empty streets. I've accomplished much more than I had anticipated. In the process, your fake laugh and deadened eyes have been archived. You've been reproduced in me, as I'm now, and I've been transformed into an acceptable replica. I don't know what I exactly need to accomplish, but I know that I have the necessary tools at my disposal. I now realize that you will always remain an actress. There's no true self to be found within you, no persona that can survive independently of one of the characters that you play. I was looking for a core that doesn't exist. You're simply a hollow Kinder Surprise that hints at some hidden depth, a miraculous prize that it can never deliver. You're the lure of the surface. Superficial seduction. I head for the hotel on St. Mark's. I'm still holding the collection of letters. Most of the papers have burnt edges. The new ones that I've written to you do not. I had planned to present them to you again in the movie theatre, a re-packaged gift from myself; this time, however, in a plain gift box. The Jackie O headband may have been too strange for your liking. But there's no use for the letters now. They're as dead to me as you are. They should really be called dead letters, poisoned letters that expired before they had a chance to live. An aborted, textual fetus. Dead at three months' gestation. They never saw the light of day.

Never took their first breath. Didn't realize their full potential.
May they rest in peace.

R.I.P.,
Adriana

SMOKE MARLBORO MENTHOLS. KEEP SMOKING BECAUSE YOUR NERVOUSNESS WILL NOT TAKE CARE OF ITSELF. AND THINK, IS THIS REALLY HAPPENING TO ME, WHEN ALL THAT I EVER WANTED WAS TO MAKE HER FEEL LIKE A STAR, TO GIVE HER A SIGN THAT SHE HAD MADE IT IN THE FILM BUSINESS, THAT SHE WAS ON TOP OF HER GAME? KNOW THAT SHE HAS TREATED YOU LIKE SHIT, DESPITE YOUR POURING YOUR HEART OUT AND YOUR SPENDING COUNTLESS HOURS ON WRITING HER THOUGHTFUL LETTERS, LEARNING ITALIAN, AND LEARNING TO PLAY DONIZETTI'S PIANO COMPOSITION. BRUTALLY REALIZE THAT YOU'RE A DISPOSABLE COMMODITY, THE CHEAPEST VERSION THERE IS, BECAUSE SHE DOESN'T WANT YOU AND DOESN'T CARE FOR YOU AT ALL. LOOK AT HER, DIRECTLY, IN THE EYES. RECOGNIZE THAT SHE WAS NEVER WHOM YOU THOUGHT SHE WAS, THAT SHE WAS JUST PLAYING YOU, AND THAT YOU FELL FOR IT, YOU STUPID LOVE-SICK FOOL. EXIT THE FILM FORUM. FEEL THE GAZE OF THE CROWD ON YOU. APPRECIATE THAT YOU'VE BEEN AT LEAST SUCCESSFUL IN SOMETHING BECAUSE THE CROWD THINKS THAT YOU'RE THAT BITCH WHOM YOU THOUGHT YOU LOVED. KEEP WALKING TO FIGURE OUT WHAT YOU NEED TO DO NOW BECAUSE, AS YOU SEE IT, YOUR LIFE IS OVER, SINCE YOU'VE NEVER CARED FOR ANYONE AS MUCH AS YOU DID FOR HER, AND SHE HAS JUST TRASHED YOU AND MADE YOU FEEL LIKE SHIT AND, ON TOP OF THAT, HAS ACCUSED YOU OF BEING HER STALKER. THINK ABOUT KILLING HER BECAUSE, IF YOU CAN'T CONTINUE LIVING, THEN SHE SHOULDN'T EITHER SINCE SHE HAS MESSED UP YOUR LIFE, COMPLETELY FUCKED IT UP, AND YOU DIDN'T DO ANYTHING WRONG. CONTEMPLATE YOUR OTHER OPTIONS. BUT REALIZE THAT THERE ARE NO OTHER OPTIONS, BECAUSE IN LOVE, WAR IS THE ONLY OPTION, AND IT ALWAYS HAS BEEN, BECAUSE

LOVE IS A BATTLEFIELD. SMOKE YOUR LAST CIGARETTE. TELL YOURSELF THAT WHEN THE LAST ASH FALLS, YOU WILL HAVE MADE A DECISION AND THAT DECISION WOULD BE FINAL, NO MATTER WHAT THE REPERCUSSIONS. FOR WHATEVER REASON, IN THAT MOMENTOUS INSTANT, THINK ABOUT ADRIEN, THAT BOY YOU SAW IN THE TOYOTA CAMRY THAT DAY WHEN YOU EXITED THE SUPERMARKET. WRITE A NOTE IN WHICH YOU GIFT HIM WITH SOMETHING, HOWEVER INDIRECTLY, TO LET HIM KNOW, IF THINGS GET OUT OF CONTROL, THAT YOUR LIFE AMOUNTED TO SOMETHING, THAT HE AND YOU WERE LINKED IN SOME WAY, AND THAT, IN THOSE SECONDS WHEN YOUR EYES CONNECTED, YOU NOW REALIZE THE PURPOSE FOR WHICH YOU WERE BORN. IN SOME WAY, SIGNAL TO HIM THAT YOU LOVED HIM MORE THAN ANYONE, MORE THAN THAT ICE-COLD BITCH, BECAUSE HE AND YOU, TOGETHER, ARE REALLY THE SAME INDIVIDUAL, IN DIFFERENT BODIES, HOLDING THE SECRET TO EACH OTHER'S DESTINIES. SOMEHOW RELAY THIS MESSAGE TO HIM BEFORE IT'S TOO LATE.

REEL (Volume 3, Issue 2) [Excerpt]

Review of Lucianetti's *In the Thanatorium*

Tessla Ferrara's latest film premiered earlier this month at the SoHo International Film Festival. It is the last installment of the trilogy of films exploring the relationship between neurological illness and the notion of the "uncanny," as explored by the Italian director, Domenico Lucianetti. (Mr. Lucianetti's previous films were *Prosopagnosia* and *Simulacri.*) *In the Thanatorium* is the final installment and, in terms of cinematography and film theory, the best crafted and most intricate. The film is shot in black and white, 8 mm film. It appears stylishly grainy, which invokes a sense of desolation and emptiness. A "thanatorium" is a place of repose or confinement before one's inevitable death. The film uses the setting of a hospice in narrating a tale of a successful actress, Vittorina, as played by Ferrara herself, who succumbs to a strange neurological illness. The disease is Creutzfeld-Jacob disease (CJD), which leaves her demented, epileptic, and ataxic (a scientific term for "imbalance"). A variant of CJD is the mad-cow disease, but the doctors in the film tell us that Vittorina's is caused by a genetic mutation of a protein, causing progressive death of the brain's nerve cells. Nevertheless, scenes of ataxic cows that are unable to stand upright are juxtaposed against Vittorina's symptoms of imbalance, creating a sense of filmic "shock," in a Benjaminian sense.

A moral dichotomy is established between the hedonistic life that Vittorina has led up to that point as a successful actress in Italy and the life she now endures in the thanatorium. As viewers, we are led down her precipice into the deterioration that she suffers daily, as she atavistically regresses to a child. In a moment of complete diegetic rupture that has been produced so well by Hitchcock, most notably in *Psycho*, where Marion, the viewer's principal protagonist, is brutally stabbed in the shower by Norman Bates, we see the actress hung in her room in a successful suicidal attempt, having understood her inevitable demise. The viewer is blindsided. Vittorina's body is subsequently transported to the medical school in Bologna to be used for teaching medical students. In the last half of the film, the viewer has no choice but to transfer her libidinal investment to another character in the film, Adriano, a medical student who, in the course of his dissection of the actress's body, falls bitterly in love with her. Thus, in the form of the dissection laboratory, we encounter another "thanatorium," where our new protagonist is being tormented for the agony he continues to experience during the dissection of his loved one. The film, suddenly, takes a very strange turn when Adriano (continued on p. 23)

"Dying
Is an art, like everything else.
I do it exceptionally well."

—Sylvia Plath
"Lady Lazarus"

"A woman must create a sense of surprise, she must fascinate..."

—Charles Baudelaire
Le Peintre de la vie moderne

The Final Cut

Without Anesthesia

Poor Soul,

I try to feel what you feel and have felt, but I possibly cannot. I
visualize. The contours of your face that were once familiar to me
have receded. I can no longer feel your matted, curly hair. But I
need to. Your small breasts call to me. They are foreign objects,
yellow fat underneath, which I have repeatedly dissected, but they
still remain mysterious to me. You are still an enigma, but I need
you so much. I need to feel you. Today, I decided, after a lengthy
and agonizing deliberation taking months, to become you. Yes, you
understand correctly. I am changing my persona, my identity, to
reflect yours. I will no longer be Adrien, but Tess. No longer man,
but woman. For this, there is so much work to be done. My father
has long ago disowned me. There would be no more shame for
him. I will need to transfer to another medical school and start
over. I will need extensive operations and medical interventions.
Plastic surgery, endocrinology, gynecology. They all end in a
"y." And I ask myself this, "Why?" To feel you better Tess, my
Narkissa besides my Narkisso. Today, I have decided to become
you no matter what the consequences. I need to feel you better. It
is better to be you, than to waste away in this pathetic state. I will
be metamorphosing to a face and body that I have learned so well.
New face, new lips, new breasts. Goodbye, Tess. You shall live in
me.

Love,
Adrien, Your New Tess

SHE TURNS ON THE IGNITION in her 1991 Honda Civic. The cold air bites her from the outside. It is such a lonely place, this car. She wonders how she ever wound up like this. Hopeless. She had such great potential. She had such a promising future. Her many instructors had told her so. She had aspired to be a critic for a contemporary film journal. School and work seem like such remote possibilities now.

She thinks of her loving parents. Of her 12 year old brother who looks up to her. She sheds tears. Hopes that they will think of the better years, past. It is such a tragic play, her life. Why did the page have to turn on her so? She's not worth a damn thing, she thinks. She has been wasted.

She is somewhere else now. She can't recall ever seeing such a majestic view. She is to be awarded a Purple Heart for the wounds she has suffered in combat in the past months. But, instead, the picture of a metal heart emerges. General George Washington carries it to her, rips her chest open, and exchanges the beating heart for this. It is 1782. It is the Revolutionary War in Newburgh, New York. She is on the Cutter, a fast sailing vessel with two masts. The force of the wind is too strong for her. She feels around her head to adjust the black monofilament wig for the camera. She needs to look good. She can't feel the rough, wavy texture. Instead, she feels smoothness, a skull that is softer than anything she has touched.

Ms. Tessla Ferrara, General George Washington's wife, the "Italian" as she is called, comes to her, dressed in an underbust corset, and leads her down the plank. The Italian holds a leather whip and orders: Follow them, those mannequins. Poison perfume reeks from the Italian's body and the smell of stale cigarette smoke from her mouth. The Italian trails behind her, brandishing her whip, as she follows nude, hairless mannequins that drop into the water, one after another. One of the mannequins turns around to photograph her. She will need to be photographed before she plunges into the water to turn into fish, this mannequin tells her. Her origins need to be documented. The Italian has demanded it. So this has been her destiny all along. Her calling. To have been born as human, to have been harvested as fish for food, to be one day cut.

Fragments of Damaged Life:
The Collected Papers of Anton Gadomsky*
(Excerpt)

Let it die. Let it die, the voice kept saying. My conscience was always talking to me and had done so since birth, in that shit-hole of an apartment. Let this love die, the voice continued: she does not love you for who you are; she loves your sickness. Isn't that what you've always wanted, Anton? The voice wouldn't shut up. Hadn't shut the fuck up for the last 77 years. Well, isn't it? The sickness?

I unexpectedly stumbled upon this Kingdom of Love in New Milford, Connecticut in the guise of Claudio Zamorano. The performance was probably my worst, like Mother's. Much too theatrical, a little too unbelievable, but not for Tess who wanted to love. I felt her sympathy when she first laid hands on me, palpating my sickly abdomen with her icily tender hands. I could tell that my colostomy bag repulsed her. Who wouldn't be repulsed? But she didn't turn away like so many others who give their superficial sympathy. She wanted to give more, and I could feel that. Her petrified hands warmed up as she kept feeling my every organ. I was awake, but I wanted that heart-felt touch so badly. I didn't let on and kept my eyes closed.

Initially, I had meant to deceive her. This was true. I could tell that she was not a seasoned medical student and played it for all that it was worth. I laid on my thick Romanian accent, and my costume was mismatched. Very bohemian. It resembled a botched gown that Mother had once made. Not for once did Tess think that

---

*   Edited and Foreword by Daniel Rubenstein, M.D., <u>Fragments of Damaged Life: The Collected Papers of</u> Anton Gadomsky Prometheus Press (Los Angeles: 1999)

this was faked, that this was staged for her. She was so intent on believing. Day after day, I felt that she was yearning to learn my every gesture, my every sickness, my every outpouring. She couldn't wait for the floodgates of emotion to open, my Tess. She was always on the verge of tears. She wore her heart on her sleeve and was continually trying to read my heart. Ha! As if mine were an open book.

But I could tell that Tess was becoming a part of me, a part of my story, and she wanted to read me so badly. I could feel her intensity, her desire. She was so different from the others. She felt so much for a woman of her age. And her appearance. She wasn't exactly a beauty queen or really feminine, although you could tell that she was trying too hard to become this. The way she would touch her hair made me feel so sorry for her. Her bangs were a little too short and she kept trying to lengthen them by pulling them down her large forehead. As if that would help. She could've used some help in the beauty department, I must admit, but I was beginning to love her all the same.

I had initially only planned to stay in this hospital in New Milford until I had recovered from the self-induced pneumothorax. But seeing Tess every day, seeing the love that she gave to me freely without asking for anything in return, made me question whether I should really leave the hospital. I wanted her next to me at all times, the mother that I never really had. For me, Tess was a drug now, a slow drug that I couldn't get out of my system. Syrup of ipecac or charcoal was of no use against this slow drug of love that bore itself through me, slower and more powerfully each day that I spent with her.

I resolved to make myself sicker. This was not in the script. I had never overstayed my hospital visits. I remembered Mother's famous saying whenever she was faced with the possibility of eviction from our apartment:

"Fish and guests smell after three days." So she had resolved to avoid this scenario of the visiting houseguest at all costs by buttering up to Ms. Walker. But this was different. Tess didn't mind my sickly smell. In fact, she breathed it as if it were a part of her. "Could she be my calling into this Kingdom of Love?" I asked myself.

I was thinking of a way out, to stay in this hospital longer, for Tess, for myself. My props were always at hand, but I was improvising this next scene with nothing in my possession, save my dagger that father had given to me on my 16th birthday. I was looking to prolong my hospital stay as much as possible without actually dying, although I knew that this would be a possibility. At that moment, I would've done anything for Tess, even if death was a consequence. She had truly become a drug that I couldn't detox.

So I opted to infect myself, to inoculate myself with anything at my disposal. It would have been easier to simply drink rat poison, as I had done in the past, to make myself bleed internally and urinate blood. I had used this strategy so often in the past, especially with novice medical students, who had not learned that rat poison is an anticoagulant, causing all sorts of internal bleeding. That's how rats die, dear students, from internal bleeding. I have learned a lot from rats in my days. They are scavengers, these rodents, eating small bits of food to make sure it's not poisonous before they feed again. The rat poison is tasteless, odorless, and takes a while to work, so they continue to nibble until they die. The voice starts up again. My conscience. Telling me to let it die. Tess is your poison, it says. You'll eat and eat of her goodness, the poisonous food that you think is so edible, until you hemorhage [sic] your heart out. The voice, it may have been right, but I couldn't stop eating.

So there was nothing in sight and I had to infect myself. I had forgotten about my damned colostomy bag with its feces. This would do, I thought. I could inject the feces in my bloodstream and cause sepsis. It would be days before the doctors could detect the source of the infection and I would be closer to Tess during those days. It didn't matter if I was consciously aware of her presence. The sepsis would certainly not allow any interactions between us. But the thought of being with my loved one, that alone would sustain me.

It was all done very fast. I had always rehearsed and calculated my scenes methodically, but this circumstance did not allow me much freedom. I became sick quite quickly and was taken to the ICU. Beyond that, I cannot recall much. I could feel Tess's presence close-by and I even thought I had smelled her scent, her unusual muskiness during those days. I imagine it was at least a week before I started feeling well again. The doctors were all ecstatic. They didn't want another skeleton like me dying on them. Tess had come to me as a vision in white. She had even had her silly, white mask on. Always so careful and so conscious of the need and safety of others. As each day passed, I realized that I loved her more and couldn't live without her.

That was the last day I spoke to her. I found out that several days later she was admitted to the ICU, the room opposite to mine even, with sepsis. You cannot imagine what horrors my mind was battling at that instant. My heart was beating so rapidly, and I was exhaling way too fast. I was in the midst of a panic attack, something that I had never experienced before. This was not staged. I was truly becoming sick. At that moment, the nurses administered some Valium to me that I have continued to take since.

I was soon discharged from the hospital, sicker than when I had first entered and now with a true illness. I was beyond broken, beyond repair. Tess continued to occupy my mind and I resolved to find a way to return to her. I had never returned to the same hospital twice for fear of being found out for my showmanship, but I had to take this gamble. For my dear love, Tess, I had to.

IT WAS WRITTEN IN THE SCRIPT. One or both of them would go. This dangerous game of cat and mouse that had lasted these months would soon end. They had played each other out. She eyed Zamorano, her Savior, who had led her to this precipice, and anticipated his next move. The dagger was laid on the tray, the dirty dagger that he carried and hid, always, in his side pocket. The objects remained the same, the pole where the IV fluid hung, the gurney, the side of which was discolored. The lights were even flickering. No one had bothered to fix them. Yes, the objects remained the same, but it was all so uncanny. She thought of Freud at this moment and the theories he espoused of the uncanny. Of the old Tess, of the identity that she had stolen from her. Of what he had once written to her about hysteria, as Adrien, in his letters to her when he was dissecting her body.

She was seeing this old man now for the first time as courageous. No longer victim, Zamorano's eyes shone with a purpose. He knew exactly what he wanted and was no longer intent in playing out this role that was thrust upon him. The old man knew. It all had happened very quickly, but Tess was encapsulating every moment as if she were documenting a bygone era that she had managed to miraculously glimpse and record. His every glance, every flickering of the lights, she was able to coordinate together. In these very seconds, she recalled her old self, as Adrien, on a hunting expedition with his father. The sequences were just as fast, but she was looking at this wolf, this man, directly. She was no longer sympathetic toward him, recognizing the fake wolf's cloak that concealed all the lies within. But she was in awe of him for having revealed this to her, this thing for which she had had no name before, of leading her astray only to find herself as she was not. She had rid herself of herself and, for this, she was grateful to him.

It was very quick, but she remembered every word as if it were her last words. He had said that he had no choice but to seduce her because he was born with this, that this was who he was. That he had played this role for years because no one had truly cared if he didn't. He had been typecast as the stage actor who acted his roles brilliantly, often dramatically, until the audience realized that they were the same gestures, the same messages, cloaked in different dialogues and scenery. He would then move from one place to another to find other audiences who would fall for his charm. But she had changed him, he said. She had shown him true love, a love that he himself could now bestow on her. His eyes were glassy now, a film having covered his blue pupils. Tears then fell like ink from his eyes as if ready to write what could not be spoken all of these years.

At that moment, on the brink of the precipice, she realized that she was no different from this stage actor. She, too, had played the role for which she was destined, for which she was cast. She had yearned to feel Zamorano's illness, his soul, only to realize that this was fake. That they were both competing for that which could never be attained, this genuine sick role, simulated again and again and perpetually fostered by their actions.

They needed each other. Could not exist without one another. She had deceived him, too, with her unsolicited lies and disguise. She had told him that much, told him about her old identity as Adrien, and that brief, devastating confession, for which he had no words, was enough for him to realize his next move. At that moment, he stripped himself bare, quickly rising to the gurney and lying there. He was ashamed of his body, so he hid his body parts under the sheets, one by one, as if each piece were separate and detachable.

When Tess had first laid eyes on his body, she had thought his body distorted and abominable. It was truly botched like Frankenstein's monster, the white and edematous skin annexed to a colostomy bag. She had felt so sorry for him and wanted to feel his pain. She would be like De Lacey, taking in a monster who had had no home and whom everybody had deemed an outcast. She had believed him and only now realized that this belief was a belief in herself as well, so that she could feel as he was feeling.

But she was wrong. He hadn't felt before and his feelings were submerged in a pool of deception.

Upon the gurney, he took that dirty dagger to his chest and stabbed himself in the sternum, again, again, and again, until the heart was punctured, until it tamponaded. It was so fast but Tess had captured the infinitesimal moments, matters, and memories until they became a part of her, recorded, and archived. He had no last words, nothing to hold on to. The dagger had fallen to the floor.

Tess had uttered no words either, an actor who had chanced upon the scene, without a role. The old man's dramatic life was reduced to this nothingness and, although there was no dying monologue, his death, she realized, would be seen as the ultimate role, the role *par excellence*. He would be forever emblazoned in the hospital's history, his symptoms and diagnoses recounted for medical students and residents alike. Yet Tess knew that this was no textbook medicine, that this act was genuine, organic.

Tess realized that this was to be her last act as well, that her entire life had led to this, would be distilled in this. To her, Zamorano was now more than a patient, more than an experiment in which she had partaken. She had authentically felt what he had felt before his last sighless gasp. She had been an actor, too, but she cried, cried, for the first time, for him as an individual in need of love, for the lies that she had told herself, for the deceptions that she had concocted, for the person whom she thought she should be.

It was late now. The din of the hospital had died. She would soon die, too. She grasped that dirty dagger, layers of blood dripping from it. There would be hordes of bacteria on it, so septic. Tess thought about this, the germs proliferating in her again. Her emerging breasts heaved ever so slightly. She had been so calm through it all.

So this is death, she thought. When she least expected it, when she least wanted it, in this way.

STEADY THE SYRINGE. ATTEMPT TO INJECT YOURSELF WITH INSULIN SO THAT YOU CAN SIMULATE ANOTHER SEIZURE. HEAR THE VOICE, SOMEWHERE IN YOUR CONSCIENCE, WHICH TELLS YOU THAT YOU WILL CONTINUE TO PLAY THE ROLE OF THE SICK PATIENT. RECOGNIZE THAT YOU LOVE THAT GIRL WITH THE STRANGE FOREHEAD AND HAIRCUT, AND THAT YOU SHOULD TELL HER YOUR SECRET, THE ONE THAT YOU'VE KEPT TO YOURSELF FOREVER. SHE WILL WALK INTO YOUR ROOM, UNEXPECTEDLY. SHE WILL SURPRISE YOU. SHE WILL UNDERSTAND THAT YOU WERE FAKING IT ALL ALONG, THAT YOU ARE NOT WHOM SHE THOUGHT YOU WERE. SHE WILL CRY AND SCREAM, BECAUSE THIS ALL MEANT SO MUCH TO HER. GO TO HER. TOUCH HER. TELL HER THAT YOU LOVE HER. SHE WILL BE QUIET, THINKING OF WHAT TO SAY NEXT. SHE WILL SEE YOUR DAGGER ON THE HOSPITAL TRAY. REMAIN SILENT FOR A WHILE. SHE WILL FINALLY TALK. SHE WILL TELL YOU THAT SHE ALSO DECEIVED YOU. SHE WILL ALSO TELL YOU THAT SHE WAS ACTUALLY A MAN BEFORE SHE MET YOU AND UNDERWENT SURGERY TO BECOME A WOMAN. YOU WILL BOTH REMAIN SILENT BECAUSE NONE OF YOU KNOWS HOW TO CONTINUE. GLANCE AT THE DAGGER. KNOW THAT YOU CAN'T CONTINUE LIKE THIS, THAT YOU ARE NOW THE ONE THAT HAS BEEN PLAYED AND THAT, DESPITE YOUR LOVE FOR HER, YOUR ROLES HAVE BEEN REVERSED SINCE SHE HAS BOTH DECEIVED YOU AND FOUND YOU OUT FOR THE PERSON WHOM YOU ARE. GRAB THE DAGGER. FEEL ITS CORRUGATED EDGES, ESPECIALLY THE LETTER A THAT HAS BEEN INSCRIBED ON IT. DON'T BE RELUCTANT. QUICKLY AND REPEATEDLY STAB YOURSELF IN THE CHEST, IN THE AREA OF YOUR HEART, BECAUSE, AFTER ALL, YOU'RE A PERFORMER AND WHAT IS MORE DRAMATIC THAN DYING LIKE OTHELLO WHEN HE, TOO, STABBED AND KILLED HIMSELF WITH A DAGGER?

The Daily Norse

Valhalla, NY
January 18, 1996

The body of a young woman was found yesterday in a 1991 Honda Civic. The victim has been identified as Adriana Eyre, 20 years of age. She was a sophomore at the State University of New York, Albany, majoring in film studies. It appears that she may have died from asphyxiation due to carbon monoxide inhalation. This was an apparent suicide, after she self-inflicted trauma to her brain. Friends at the University tell us that she was recently undergoing a bout of major depression after she was denied an interview with one of her favorite actresses, Tessla Ferrara. Through sources yet to be disclosed, she had been stalking Ferrara for a brief period of time and had even tried to imitate her in appearance. She is survived by her parents and younger brother. The victim's body is to be donated to New York Medical College, here in Valhalla, as previously designated by Adriana Eyre herself.

As she was exiting the hospital room, Death's high-heeled pumps caught the dirty dagger on the floor and she slipped. Death wasn't used to her shoes yet. Fuck, she thought, this day isn't going well, not as she had planned. First, the girl's death and now this. Her left heel had broken as well. It really was much easier, all of it, with her black robe and scythe. But, no, she had to play and pretend that she was something that she wasn't. She was being penalized for her deceptions. She picked up her broken-heeled corseted black shoe, and limped to the door. Her black wig was itching her head as well. She took this off and threw it on the floor. This is someone else's problem now.

He had tried to be so good lately and finish someone else's work, and this is how he got treated! No thanks. Dinner was waiting for him. But when would he tell his wife, who had no suspicion that he was masquerading himself as her, going on a month's death spree, with that black chiffon scarf of hers? His adventure would end today. He would have to occupy himself with the death ledgers again, that tedious task for which he would trade anything. Death opened the door as he once was and exited. He knew how the end always is.

Lights out

Acknowledgements

Numerous people—too many to all name here—have been involved with the publication of this book—some for support and inspiration, some for insightful critiques, and some for the actual production. Whatever their roles, all are greatly appreciated and have made this novel a reality.

First, I would like to wholeheartedly thank and acknowledge Debra Di Blasi, the publisher and editor-in-chief of Jaded Ibis Press, without whom the publication of this book would not be possible. She has been exceptional and invaluable in her wisdom and intellectual prowess, and has been an ardent supporter throughout the book's publication. I am grateful for what she has done for this book and for me, personally and professionally. She is a truly kind and unique individual, and I could not ask for a better publisher-in-chief or publishing company.

Second, I wish to express deep and undying gratitude to my various family members, both near and far, who have supported me emotionally while writing this book. In particular, I would like to thank my parents, the Navab, Rashidi, Saadat-Fard, and Shamloo families, my numerous cousins here in LA and Toronto, and especially my twin sister, Pooneh, whose courageousness, wisdom, and infinite kindness serve as continual reminders of love and a robust support system.

I would also like to avow my appreciation for friends who have provided astute comments about this novel. In particular, I would like to thank Mariam Beevi, Rosalind Galt, Lisa Lutz, and Nicole Rizzuto, who were generous enough to read the manuscript and offer their insights.

Yalda and Houda Zakeri also deserve great recognition for their willingness to collaborate with me in the production of this book. Not only are they extremely talented individuals who completed the illustration and musical scores of this novel, respectively, but they are also friends whom I've known since childhood. Sincere thanks to them both.

Persons who have been instrumental in allowing me time and latitude to create artistically, without any limits and with much encouragement, include Julie Handelman and Nurit Grunfeld. They and their families have been my strongest supporters inside and outside work.

My talent agent, Carrie Macy at AC Talent (Next Management), deserves recognition for representing me in commercial modeling work and allowing me to pursue an avenue outside of my main occupation as a neurologist.

Other friends who have been instrumental in their support and camaraderie through the years of writing this novel include—and by no means is this list comprehensive---Ana Bidoglio, Heather Burbank, Janelle Caywood, Charles Chatelain, Sandra Cho, Gwynne Church, Cameron and Liz Compton, Angie and Jason Cook, Marc Davidson, Candy and Rene Fuentes, Chris Gaul, Evelina Gentry, Vida Ghaffari, Keith O. Gonzalez, Paul Han, Karyn Ihara, Jay and Grace Kwee, Mai Le, Jean Lin, Marcus and Rachel Loo, Mitra Memari, Maryam and Mojdeh Mohaghegh, Camillo Morganti, Sansan Lin Murray, Tara Nader, Rachael Noguera, Michael Pobanz, Roxana Pourshalimi, Elizabeth Quinn, Shruti Rana, Siva Reddy, Marc Rezvani, Farhad Sarmadi, Daniela and Franco Saspe, Abbi and Anthea Sefa-Boakye, Sahar Sedadi, Rich Silva, Farid Tamjidi, Steve and Jenne Thomson, Myrka Torres, Cherie Turner, Olga Uchima, Ioana Urma, Tamar Yeghiayan, Kim Wayte, and Daryl and Serena Wong.

Lastly, I would like to thank my numerous instructors who provided the impetus for critical thinking and writing, and proved to be a great source of inspiration for this novel. Rey Chow has been a guiding force and mentor since my undergraduate years, and her vitality and friendship never cease to impress me. Stuart Culver taught me to enjoy literature, while allowing me to also think critically while writing. I thank him for allowing me to recognize the need to write fiction intelligently and critically. During my fellowship years at Stanford, I would like to sincerely thank Steve Brooks, Anstella Robinson, and Rafael Pelayo, who made medical education so appealing and also entertaining. At Loyola, I was fortunate enough to encounter Tracey Freed, Gary Gelfand, James Gilliam, Hope Levy-Biehl, Elizabeth Pollman, David Steele, Marcy Strauss, Georgene Vairo, and Paul Von Blum who continue to be good friends and supporters of my work.

My sincere gratitude extends to each of them.

About the Author

Pedram Navab is a neurologist and sleep medicine specialist who currently resides in Los Angeles. Educated at Stanford and Brown universities, he also holds a graduate degree in English/Modern Culture & Media and a J.D.

About the Artist

Yalda Zakeri is an artist by trade, having earned her BFA from Rhode Island School of Design, and has spent her professional career working in the advertising industry. She currently lives in San Francisco where she creates art for special projects and works as a freelance art director/designer.

Made in the USA
San Bernardino, CA
09 November 2015